"What are you doing up here anyway?"

Isabel turned, her expression filled with challenge.

If they were going to get out of this mess, Jason needed her to trust him. "I'm with the law—that's all you need to know."

She bent forward with her arms folded over her chest. "He thinks we're partners."

"What?"

She stopped and stared at the sky. "When he held that knife to my throat, he accused us of working together to steal his fortune."

"Really?" Maybe he could still salvage this investigation. As long as the thief didn't think he was connected to law enforcement. "I'm sorry about the knife."

She shrugged. "It wasn't you that did it." She did a double take as though she were trying to ferret out some hidden motive in him or see beneath his skin.

She still didn't trust him.

Isabel stared up at the house, her voice filled with worry. "Maybe he'll just go away."

Jason doubted that.

Ever since she found the Nancy Drew books with the pink covers in her country school library, **Sharon Dunn** has loved mystery and suspense. Most of her books take place in Montana, where she lives with three nearly grown children and a spastic border collie. She lost her beloved husband of twenty-seven years to cancer in 2014. When she isn't writing, she loves to hike surrounded by God's beauty.

Books by Sharon Dunn

Love Inspired Suspense

Dead Ringer
Night Prey
Her Guardian
Broken Trust
Zero Visibility
Montana Standoff
Wilderness Target
Cold Case Justice
Mistaken Target
Fatal Vendetta
Big Sky Showdown
Hidden Away

Texas Ranger Holidays

Thanksgiving Protector

Witness Protection

Top Secret Identity

Texas K-9 Unit

Guard Duty

HIDDEN AWAY

SHARON DUNN

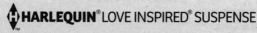
HARLEQUIN® LOVE INSPIRED® SUSPENSE

Recycling programs
for this product may
not exist in your area.

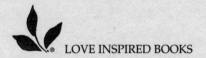 LOVE INSPIRED BOOKS

ISBN-13: 978-1-335-54381-3

Hidden Away

Copyright © 2018 by Sharon Dunn

www.Harlequin.com

Printed in U.S.A.

Remember ye not the former things, neither consider the things of old. Behold, I will do a new thing; now it shall spring forth; shall ye not know it?
—*Isaiah* 43:18-19

To my Lord, savior, friend, counselor and king.
Jesus, for more than thirty years,
we have walked this journey together.

ONE

Despite the windows being shut against winter temperatures, a chill skittered across detective Jason Enger's skin. Hidden in the trees that surrounded the property, he stared at the monitor in his surveillance van as a man made his way toward the door of the secluded mansion.

Ten miles from the house and nestled in the Montana mountains was the town of Silver Strike. The booming tourist spot was not only a place for world-class skiing and fly-fishing, but also ground zero for an international smuggling ring. Couriers used empty vacation homes as pickup points for valuable smuggled items that were often of cultural significance to the country they'd been taken from.

As a private detective, Jason had been working with the FBI for months to identify the couriers and the buyers in hopes that one of them would lead to the mastermind behind it all. The Bureau coordinated with US Customs to track when artifacts had been stolen from museums or personal collections.

As Jason watched the man type in security codes on the keypad by the door, look around nervously and step inside, he was pretty sure he'd hit pay dirt. Figuring out how the thief had gotten the security codes was a piece of the puzzle for the Bureau to discover. Jason's job was to take photos that would lead to identifying all the players involved.

Three weeks ago, an eighteen-karat-gold bookmark that had belonged to Mussolini had been stolen from a museum in Italy. The Bureau had been watching several empty properties ever since.

Jason took a deep breath. His camera hadn't recorded a clear picture of the man's face, so he'd wait around until the perp came back out. That way he'd be sure of a positive ID. The thief had walked up to the mansion. He must have parked his car in some out-of-the-way place so it wouldn't be spotted in the driveway of a house that was supposed to be unoccupied. The falling snow would cover the man's tracks in a matter of minutes, leaving no trace.

Jason stared at the monitors. A car pulled up, and a woman stepped out. His heart beat a little faster as he leaned closer to the screen. She tilted her chin and squared her shoulders with none of the nervous body language the man had displayed. Everything about her, from her posture to the way she dressed, projected confidence and money, very Ivy League. Who was she?

The woman punched in the security codes and disappeared behind the ornate wooden door. Jason's throat went dry. Was she an innocent homeowner unexpectedly walking into a dangerous situation or was she allied with the thief?

If she was not involved, he needed to get her out of there before she crossed the thief's path. Most of the men in the crime ring who had been identified had a history of violence. The thought of harm coming to a woman made Jason's chest tight. He wrestled with indecision. He couldn't risk blowing this operation either; months of work would go down the tubes if the smuggling ring found out the Feds were onto them. Arresting the couriers would be an act of futility, since only finding the kingpin would end the syndicate.

He reached for a work shirt with the name *Mel* written on the pocket and a clipboard he kept in a tote, part of his go-to kit for his work as a PI. Walking around a neighborhood in a uniform meant most people didn't notice you. He put his zip-front hoodie and coat back on.

His chest muscles squeezed tight. He was taking a huge risk in showing himself, but a woman might get hurt if he didn't.

He pulled the van into the driveway, grabbed his gun from the glove compartment and placed it in his waistband so his winter coat covered it. He prayed he wouldn't have to use the gun. Snow cascaded and twirled from the sky as he hurried toward the door.

Usually it was easy enough for him to get a read on people. If the woman was innocent, he'd find a way to convince her to leave. If guilty, he'd get a good look at her face, assuming she would even answer the door. Not answering would be a giveaway that she was involved. It would take an Oscar-worthy performance to not give away his real reason for being here if she was in on the operation, but he was confident of his abilities.

He touched the doorbell with a gloved finger, took in a breath and prepared to play Mel the concerned county worker.

From the moment she'd stepped into the Wilsons' house, something felt off to Isabel Connor. The hairs on the back of her neck stood at attention as her heart thudded faster. She couldn't let go of the feeling that she was being watched.

She shook her head, trying to free herself of her uneasiness. Maybe it was just because the

Wilsons had chosen to show up three days earlier than expected. They'd texted her directly instead of getting in touch with her employer, Mary Helms at Sun and Ski Property Management. It was Isabel's job to get the houses ready for the clients. Stock the refrigerator, make sure the property was in working order, place fresh flowers in the vases, whatever it took to make clients feel comfortable in their vacation home.

Grabbing some books that had been left on an entryway table, she headed toward the upstairs library, stopping to turn the thermostat up a few degrees. She put the books on the shelf and then ran back downstairs to inspect the kitchen, where some papers and boxes had been left on the counter, probably by a cleaning crew. Since she still needed to unload flowers and groceries from her car, she'd left the alarm off so she could run in and out of the house quickly. She'd reset it when she left.

The doorbell rang.

Her breath caught in her throat as that gut feeling that something was off rose to the surface. Who on earth could that be? The Wilsons' house was miles from downtown Silver Strike and other homes. They hadn't been back here in months. News of the Wilsons' early arrival couldn't have gotten out that fast. Not even her boss knew the Wilsons had had a change of plans. She hurried from the kitchen but walked a little slower as she approached the front door.

Through the window by the door, she could see a man with a clipboard. Her heart raced a little faster as she swung the door open.

The man offered her a warm smile. "Afternoon, ma'am. It seems there's been a gas leak at one of the homes under construction. We're advising all nearby homeowners to vacate their premises until we can be sure there is no danger."

Though she remained calm on the surface, a hurricane of suspicion raged through her. "What construction?" Isabel managed to hide her fear by squaring her shoulders and lifting her chin. A posture she had practiced in the mirror for hours. The way she dressed and how she carried herself were pieces of the professional image she'd taught herself to project so no one would ever guess her dark past.

"Up the road. I'm with the county. This is just a precaution." There was something genuine about that smile, but she wasn't about to be taken in. Charm was an inch deep. What if this man had come to rob this place, thinking it was going to be empty, and now he was trying to get rid of her? She had a responsibility to the Wilsons.

There might be construction up the road. She

had no idea. Silver Strike was booming and people were willing to pay for building even in the winter. She knew there were other houses around here. The area was actually considered to be a subdivision, though each property was at least five acres. She angled her head to look past him. His van seemed somewhat official, though there was no logo on it.

He ran his hands through his dark hair and flashed blue eyes at her.

Trust your gut, Izzy.

She wasn't about to be dazzled by his good looks or his blue eyes. That always led to heartache. It had taken her seven long years to rebuild her life after falling for the charming petty criminal Nick Solomon when she was a teenager. Trusting a man on any level was never a good idea.

"You said it was just a precaution." She read his name tag, which was visible beneath his open coat and zip-front sweatshirt. "I'll take my chances, Mel." She lifted her hand toward the door to close it. "I have work to do."

"Work?" Now *his* voice sounded suspicious. He put his foot between the door and the frame.

The aggression of his move set off alarm bells for her. "Yes. I work for a property management company. I have to get the house ready for clients." She was pretty sure there was no gas leak. Her priority needed to be with her job. Mary Helms, the owner of Sun and Ski Property Management, had taken a chance on her in the first place. Though she'd turned her life around and over to God, Isabel had a criminal record that made employment tricky.

"Please, I think you need to leave the house... just for a short time. What is your name?"

"Isabel..." She stopped. It was none of his business who she was. She lifted her head to meet his gaze. The tone to his voice had been almost desperate. Though there was nothing plastic about his expression or the pleading look in his eyes, she was pretty sure he was up to something. He was probably just a very good actor—that was why she had doubts. Most men were good at pretending to care. "Thank you, sir, for the warning, and have a good day." She pushed the door into its frame so he had to step out of the way.

Hands shaking, heart racing, Isabel pressed against the wall by the door and took in a prayer-filled breath. What if that man meant to rob this place? She just didn't buy the gas-leak story.

I can do all things through Christ Jesus who strengthens me.

She peered through the window by the door, watching the man's van pull out of the driveway. She didn't like being here alone.

Tension coiled tight in her chest. What should she do? She hurried to the entryway table where she'd left her purse and phone. The Wilsons didn't have a landline. What if she was totally wrong? Other than her gut feeling, she really didn't have any evidence the man was up to something. It would not be good for Sun and Ski's reputation to have police swarming a client's property for no reason.

She clicked open her purse and felt for her phone. Maybe the smart thing to do would be to call her boss first.

She stepped back into the living room and stared at her phone, prepared to dial Mary's number. She hit the first number.

An arm wrapped around her waist and a knife pressed against her neck.

"So you and your partner are trying to horn in on my good fortune."

Her heart raged in her chest as her body stiffened against the prospect of having her throat slit.

The man pressed his cheek against her ear. The voice was not that of the man in the van.

Isabel jammed her elbow hard into the man's stomach. He grunted and loosened his grip on her. She twisted free of his hold and hurried toward the kitchen. She had only a few seconds' head start while the man recovered from the blow. Stepping into the large pantry of the kitchen, she slipped behind a shelf of canned goods, hoping the darkness would hide her from view. She knew the layout of the house well enough. This was probably the best hiding place on the main floor.

She'd lost her phone in the struggle. Closing her eyes, she listened to the raging of her own heartbeat, praying that the man with the knife only glanced into the dark pantry. If he left to search elsewhere, she could make a run for the door and get to her car. But she wondered if the man who had come to the door was in on this home invasion. Even if she made it to her car, she might have to deal with Mel. Her life now depended on all those what-ifs.

Isabel drew a prayer-filled breath and pressed deeper into the pantry.

Midway down the long driveway, Jason hit the brakes and listened to the engine hum. The smart thing would be to return to his hiding place and wait for the two thieves, the man and the woman who called herself Isabel, to emerge from the house, then do his job—get the photos the Bureau had hired him to take.

His job was to be invisible. If the smugglers knew they were being watched, the investigation would fall apart. In order to get to the mastermind, they had to let the petty criminals do the thefts and not involve local cops making low-level arrests.

No part of that plan made the tightness in his chest subside. He prided himself on being able to tell friend from foe. Discerning motives in people was part of what made him a good PI. Still, he was uncertain about the woman in the house. Yes, she'd given him the brush-off, but something about her had been so vulnerable, afraid even. Was she telling the truth about being the hired help or just trying to get rid of him so she and her partner could finish the job? Or maybe she'd been brought in on this against her will.

He had to know for sure.

He killed the engine and slipped out of the van, dashing toward the side of the house and pressing along the wall. The van would only be visible from upstairs north-facing windows, not from the downstairs. He crouched down beneath the window by the door and peered inside. Pieces of a shattered vase lay on the floor by the foyer table. A woman's purse was flung against the wall. Signs of a struggle?

He didn't want anyone to die here today.

Jason steeled himself and opened the door. He slipped into the dark house. Still determined not to blow this operation but to get the woman out of danger, he padded noiselessly through the foyer.

The silence on the main floor was eerie. The contents of a purse lay scattered across the ornate tile. Turning in a slow circle, he stepped over the shards from the broken vase. He scanned the main floor and then his gaze traveled up to the mezzanine and the second floor, where a creaking noise had come from.

He climbed stealthily up the stairs, his heart drumming in his ears. Once he made it to the second floor, the polished floorboards of the interior balcony didn't creak when he placed his foot on them. He hurried down the hallway, checking each room, bathroom, den, first bedroom. All empty.

Back at the mezzanine, Jason pressed against the wall and listened.

Down below, noise rose up from what was probably the kitchen. Isabel darted past his field of vision and disappeared through a door on the other side of the house. He sprinted to the top of the stairs.

A man burst out from where Isabel had come. The same tall thin man who had entered the house earlier—he glanced from side to side and then darted in the opposite direction of Isabel. He must not have seen where Isabel had gone.

Jason caught the glint of a knife in the man's hand. Okay, so maybe she was in danger.

He rushed down the stairs, keeping his step light so as not to draw attention to himself. He ran across the black-and-white tile of the open entryway toward the door where Isabel had gone.

Even before he opened the door, he smelled chlorine. The humid air of the pool room assaulted him as he stepped across the threshold. As on a game show, there were four doors to choose from. Which one had she gone through?

He tiptoed on the tile and eased open the first door. Storage. When he opened the second door, he found a bedroom. Much more promising. He checked the closet and the bathroom first, then stood beside the bed. Before he could lean over to check underneath, a hard object slammed against his shin, sending a wave of pain through his calf muscle.

With pain shooting up his leg, he knelt to pull the culprit out from underneath the bed.

TWO

Isabel knew it was predictable to hide under the bed, but she'd been in a hurry. She'd grabbed a hairbrush from the vanity before slipping under the bed frame. If she was to save herself from the man with the knife, she knew she had to attack before he found her. She was no match for him physically, but she could outsmart him.

The man groaned in pain when she hit his shin with the brush. She crawled to the other side of the bed and rolled out. Just as she got to her feet, he grabbed her from behind.

She angled her body to get away and lifted her foot to kick his calf.

"Calm down, calm down. I'm not the bad guy here."

It was Mel's smooth voice. So he'd come back. She had no idea what Mr. Knife had meant by the partner comment. Mel and Mr. Knife were probably robbing the place together.

"Be quiet." He placed a hand over her mouth. "He'll find us."

Probably a trick to get her to stop resisting. She twisted her torso and dug her fingernails into his forearm.

Still he cupped her mouth, his other arm wrapped around her waist, and held her tight against his chest. But he didn't hurt her or pull a weapon on her. She tried to twist free. He dragged her across the floor.

"Look, this place is not safe. I'll take you back to town." He guided her through the door and stepped into the pool room even as she continued to try to get away from him. He took his hand off her mouth.

"I have my own car." Like she wanted to go anywhere with this thief. She'd had enough of falling for the bad boy to last a lifetime.

She pulled free of him with so much force that she fell headlong into the pool. Cold water enveloped her. Strong arms grabbed the back of her collar and pulled her to the surface.

"Now for sure he's heard us," said Mel.

She gasped for air and reached for the edge of the pool. Mel let go of her and ran toward a door. He returned with a large towel, which he tossed toward her.

"You can't go outside like that. You'll freeze," he said. "Do these people have clothes here?"

The concern for her physical well-being gave her pause. But if he wasn't a thief, what was he doing here? She pulled herself to her feet as water dripped off her. "I can't wear a client's clothes." She picked up the towel.

He grabbed her at the elbow. "You're going to have to."

She was not keen on going anywhere with this man, but it felt like she was on a runaway train trying to stop it by dragging her feet.

Glancing around nervously, he led her through a door back out into the living room.

Her heart sank when she saw the broken vase and the mess in the entryway. Everything in this house was probably valuable. She spotted the contents of her purse on the floor, but not her phone. It must have been kicked out of view in the struggle with Mr. Knife.

"Where are the clothes?"

"Can't we just call the police?" She still didn't know what this guy's game was.

"That's a bad idea."

Her steps faltered. "Why?" What if this was a trap? He'd pretend to be helping her and then what? Kill her so he and Mr. Knife could finish the job they'd come to do?

"Trust me. We don't want the police here."

Isabel felt that familiar tightening in her

stomach. Trust him? She didn't even know him, and so far almost everything he did made her suspicious.

He grabbed her elbow and led her up the stairs. "Which room?"

Noise rose up from a side room on the main floor. She hurried toward the master suite. Glancing over the balcony as they slipped behind the door, she caught a glimpse of movement down below. Mr. Knife was still looking for her on the main floor.

Mel searched the huge room. "That closet is the size of my apartment. Change in there. I'll keep watch."

She slipped into the closet and slid the door shut. How was she going to explain wearing a client's clothes to her boss? She grabbed the least expensive-looking shirt and pants she could find. As if that would make a difference. Even telling the truth about what had gone on would sound crazy, like she was trying to cover up her strange actions with a fantastic story. Because of her history with the law, she had a fear of not being believed.

Though her brain ached over what might happen, she knew she needed to focus on the now. Getting away from Mr. Knife and maybe even

Mel. For sure, he wasn't some concerned official from the county. What was his game?

She buttoned up the shirt and then grabbed
a sweater to put over it. Actually, this closet
was bigger than her apartment. Her boss had
been kind enough to rent her the studio apartment above the Sun and Ski office. She changed
quickly and grabbed a pair of boots. Victoria
Wilson was half a size bigger than she, but the
boots would keep out the cold. Not sure what
to do with her wet clothes, she put them on a
hanger to dry. Another crazy action she'd have
to explain. She looked around for a coat but
couldn't find one.

Mel knocked on the door. "Hurry."

She slid the closet door open. Mel peered
through the slightly ajar bedroom door out into
the hallway.

He glanced in her direction, his expression
tense. "He's upstairs. Is there another way out
of here besides down the stairs and through the
front door?"

She still didn't know what to think of this
man. Friend or foe? "I suppose we could leave
by way of the balcony." She pointed. Through
the sliding glass doors, she saw that the snowfall had increased. The lazy flakes that had
fallen out of the sky when she drove up here
had turned into slashing swords.

Mel shut and locked the bedroom door. He stepped across the room and slid the balcony door open, signaling for her to follow. She hesitated.

The doorknob wiggled and then there was a thump against it.

Her heart seized up as she looked from Mel to the door.

"Come on, Isabel."

She had told him her name when she answered the door. But when he spoke it, something sparked inside her. Warm feelings aside, she still didn't know what Mel was up to. Why didn't he want to call the police?

A body thudded against the door again. And then she heard clicking noises. Mr. Knife was picking the lock.

Mel was the one without the knife. Maybe her odds were better with him. She darted through the open sliding glass door. Snow stung her skin. The cold hit her with full force, but the heavy wool sweater cut out much of it. Her wet hair seemed to freeze instantly, turning into hard straw-like strands.

"I'll lower you down. Hurry," he said.

She darted to the edge of the balcony and slipped through the wide railing. He grabbed her hands. His grip was like iron. He held on and eased her down.

The ground below her loomed closer. She looked up into Mel's blue eyes.

His expression was strained, face tight, teeth showing from the exertion. His body hung off the edge of the balcony at a dangerous angle. He strained. "I'm going to have to let you go."

She nodded. She fell through space, landing hard, her knees buckling. Mel slipped off the balcony and dropped to the ground with the grace of an Olympic gymnast. He grabbed her hand. They ran, feet pounding the fresh fallen snow.

She glanced over her shoulder just as she rounded the corner. Mr. Knife had come to the edge of the outdoor balcony. If he chose not to follow them and went back down the stairs and out the front door, it would buy them time.

As Mel pulled her around the house toward the driveway where his van was parked, she had the gut-wrenching sensation that her life was about to switch into a retread of seven years ago. Here she was again, blindly following a man who might be a criminal.

Oh Lord, please protect me.

She'd been barely seventeen when Nick Solomon decided to rob a convenience store at gunpoint. He'd kissed her in the car and told her he was going inside for a bag of chips. When he slid into the passenger seat clearly agitated and commanded her to drive, she'd done what he asked. All because she'd loved and trusted him.

They hurried toward the van. Mel kicked the front tires. "Slashed." His forehead furled. "When did he find time to do that?"

She studied him for just a moment. Maybe Mel was telling the truth. Maybe he was the good guy. She wanted to believe that. She had a feeling she was staking her life on it.

"My car looks okay." She spoke between breaths and took off running toward her car. She jumped into the driver's seat and turned the key in the ignition. Because she'd thought she would be alone at the Wilsons', she had no reason to take her keys with her.

Mel got into the passenger seat.

She clicked into Reverse and hit the gas, then spun around and pointed the car toward the snowy road.

Mel gripped the armrest. "NASCAR, here we come. Who taught you to drive like that?"

A heaviness descended on her like a shroud, and she felt that stab to her heart. Nick had taught her to drive like that. Little had she realized he was grooming her to be his getaway driver.

She stared at the road ahead. Her car slipped to one side. She checked her rearview mirror.

Mr. Knife stood in the driveway, arms crossed over his chest.

The car made a serpentine pattern and slid on the snow-covered road.

"Something is wrong here." She struggled to keep the car on the road. Even with the slick roads, steering was taking way more muscle power than usual. The car began to shake and vibrate.

"I think your tires are losing air." Mel's voice remained calm. "No way would he have time to do both cars." He studied the road and the surrounding trees as if he was trying to piece something together.

So her tires had been slashed too. Mr. Knife must have been in a hurry and not cut deep enough for the air to leak out fast.

She gripped the steering wheel as a tree loomed in front of her. The entire car seemed to be vibrating to pieces as the metallic clang of driving on her rims filled the front seat.

She scraped past the tree, but the car rammed into a smaller tree and came to an abrupt stop. Their bodies lurched forward then slammed back against the seat.

Mel craned his neck to stare out the back window.

Fear cut her to the bone. "Is he coming for us?"

"I can't see him."

Isabel tensed as she glanced over her shoulder. That didn't mean he wouldn't come after them.

"This car is not going to get us off this mountain. We're going to have to call...somebody." He pulled his phone out.

Somebody? What did that mean? Why not the police? Mr. Knife seemed to think they both were out to steal the fortune he'd come for. Whatever it was he was looking for in that house, it must be worth a great deal because Mr. Knife seemed determined that they not leave the house.

A chill ran up her spine. In fact, Mr. Knife seemed pretty bent on eliminating his perceived competition altogether. Why give him a chance at that?

Mel clicked open the door. "I can't get a signal. We can't stay out in this storm long. Maybe we can get a signal back at the house."

"Are you nuts?" she said.

"What other choice do we have here? It's five miles to the main road and another five into town. Who knows if any neighbors are home. Do you want to walk in a storm without a coat? You'll freeze to death."

She took in a breath. And it would be dark soon. He had a point. "Okay."

"You know the layout of the house, right?

There must be someplace where we could make the call and hide out."

She clicked open her door, inviting the intense wind and cold in. "Mrs. Wilson has an art studio at the back of the property."

He hurried around the car and tugged on her elbow. "Let's get into the trees. More shelter and we won't be spotted off the bat if he does come after us. Maybe I'll be able to pick up a signal before we get to the house."

She doubted that, not with the storm brewing. She crossed her arms over her chest and put her head down. She had no choice but to go with Mel's plan. Even the short walk back to the house was going to leave her chilled to the bone at the very least.

The trees cut the wind and the snow by a little bit. They'd tromped only a short distance before the cold settled into her bones. Mel slipped out of his coat and placed it on her shoulders. She could still feel the warmth of his body heat as she put her arms in the sleeves.

The gesture warmed her heart too. The front-zip sweatshirt he had over his uniform shirt couldn't provide much more warmth than her borrowed sweater.

"I'll be all right. I got my thermals on." He offered her a smile that brought a sparkle into his eyes. Beautiful blue eyes.

Don't be taken in, Izzy.

One small act of kindness did not reveal a man's whole character. "So you're not really with the county, are you?"

"No." He pressed his lips together and stared straight ahead, making it clear he wasn't going to tell her anything else. "The less you know, the better."

More secrecy.

As they forged through the quiet forest, Isabel felt a heaviness descend on her. What was God doing here? It felt like she was losing everything she'd fought for from the moment she'd given Him her heart in that jail cell. Her job was in jeopardy, her car had been sabotaged and she may be hooked up with another criminal.

Mel brushed the snow out of his hair. "We'll get this straightened out. Trust me."

She didn't fail to notice the flatness in his voice as if he was trying to convince himself that everything was going to be okay.

Trust me. Those were some famous last words. Wind gusted and swirled through the trees. Isabel zipped the borrowed coat up to her neck and prayed that Mel was right.

As he trudged through the snow, Jason's thoughts raced faster than a horse a mile from the barn. He glanced over at Isabel. Soft honey-colored curls covered her face as she bent forward to shield herself from the falling, blowing snow. She was pretty. He'd at least admit that.

She seemed innocent enough, but something about her just didn't ring true.

The thief hadn't found the bookmark yet or he would have left. Maybe the thief thought he or Isabel had it and that was why he was bent on taking them out. The guy was a fool to come after them. He wouldn't be utilized again by the mastermind. Whoever was orchestrating the smuggling had kept it very under the radar. These low-level guys were sometimes more brawn than brains.

The one thing he knew for certain was that he couldn't let this investigation fall apart. The agents at the Bureau had put in hundreds of labor hours to gather profiles of all the people involved. His job was just one small part of a bigger picture.

Once he got a signal, he'd call his contact at the Bureau to come and get them. He'd tell Isabel the guy was a friend. The less she knew, the safer she was.

A chill had settled on his skin and was making its way to his bones. He didn't regret giving his coat to Isabel, though. His father had taught him to be a gentleman. A lot of good it had done his dad. The man had endured a difficult marriage only to have his mom leave for another man. After the end of his own bad relationship, Jason had concluded that if women weren't cheaters, they were liars. Isabel might not be a thief, but she was still hiding something. He just wasn't sure what.

While they were working their way back to the house, he might as well try to figure out why she seemed to be acting a part.

"So how long have you worked for this property management place?" The trees thinned and he caught a glimpse of the obnoxiously big house with its central dome.

"What are you doing up here, anyway?" She turned, her expression filled with challenge.

If they were going to get out of this mess, he needed her to trust him. "I'm with the law. That's all you need to know."

She bent forward with arms folded over her chest. "He thinks we're partners."

"What?"

She stopped and stared at the sky. "When he held that knife to my throat—" She lifted her chin and squared her shoulders, but her quivering mouth revealed she was upset.

His emotions whiplashed from rage that a man would be so violent toward a woman to compassion for Isabel. "It's not right that happened to you."

As quickly as she had lost it, she regained her composure. "Anyway, he accused us of working together to steal his fortune."

Maybe he could still salvage this investigation. As long as the thief didn't think he was connected to law enforcement. "I'm sorry about the knife."

She shrugged. "It wasn't you that did it." She did a double take as though she were trying to ferret out some hidden motive in him or see beneath his skin.

She still didn't trust him.

The trees thinned.

Isabel stared up at the house, her voice filled with worry. "Perhaps he'll just go away."

He doubted that.

"He made a mess in the foyer," she said. "If we get out of here, I'll have to explain that to my clients and my boss."

Her priorities seemed a little out of order. "Let's just focus on getting out of here before he has a chance to come after us again." His phone still showed no signal.

Snow pelted them as they came out in the open and approached the circular driveway. "Hide behind my van. He might be watching."

He didn't want to worry Isabel. She seemed anxious enough, but another thought concerned him. How did the man with the knife have time to slash both sets of tires and come after them pretty much nonstop? He suspected there was not one but two thieves roaming around the estate. One of them had probably been waiting in the unseen car and been called in when things fell apart.

Isabel scurried up the driveway and crouched on the far side of the van. He slipped in beside her, leaning close to whisper in her ear. "Let's figure out where he is before we go to that studio. Is there a back way in?" Though he didn't want to alarm Isabel, he wanted to know if they were dealing with not one but two men.

She nodded. "Through the kitchen."

She led him around the house using the bushes for cover, then opened a door to a kitchen fit for a four-star restaurant. Stainless steel gleamed everywhere. An array of pots and pans hung above the island. The granite countertop displayed every gadget and more appliances than anyone could utilize in their lifetime. The lights were out. Clouds covered the late-day sun, making the room dim.

Isabel rushed toward the swinging kitchen door. He peered through it at the open living room and expansive entryway with its black-and-white checked floor.

If the thief was watching any part of the house, it had to be the entryway. The second-story mezzanine provided a bird's-eye view of the main floor. The man with the knife could stand in the shadows and wait for them to cross the space. Jason studied each inch of the second floor as much as his limited view would allow. And if the thief had an accomplice, that only created more land mines.

Still no signal on his phone. The storm might be messing things up. He was going to need warmer clothes, or at least a coat, if they had to go back outside.

He cupped a hand on her shoulder. "You stay here. It'll be safer. I'm going to see if I can figure out exactly where those guys are."

"Guys?" she whispered.

He put his finger to his lips and signaled for her to stay.

He eased open the door. Keeping an eye on the second floor, he pressed his back against the textured wall. The whole house seemed darker. He wondered if the storm had taken out the electricity.

Jason's heart pounded wildly. He loved this part of his job. Most detective work involved sitting and watching the sordid lives of other people. As dangerous as the situation was, he couldn't help but relish the excitement.

He slipped into the living room, staying in the shadows and watching for movement. Gaze darting everywhere. Listening for the slightest out-of-place noise.

He waited for some time. No chance that these guys had just left. One of them might be searching the woods for them. The other looking for the bookmark they'd come here for.

Jason eased open the door and stepped back into the kitchen. His heart seized up.

Isabel wasn't there.

Heart racing, he opened the door to the pantry. When he tried the light switch, it didn't work. He whispered her name and circled through the pantry. No answer. He doubted she'd wandered off. Most likely, she'd been chased or…taken at knifepoint.

Either way, he needed to find her and fast.

THREE

Once again, Mr. Knife pressed the metal blade against Isabel's neck. He'd dragged her through the kitchen and into the media room on the far side of the house. Lighting strips marked the aisles between rows of chairs. A single light that must be battery operated blazed on the back wall, lighting the media equipment.

She could feel the cold blade against her skin. She cringed, envisioning that coppery smell and the warm seeping of her own blood.

Oh God, I don't want to die.

Mr. Knife leaned close and spoke in her ear, his voice raspy and filled with venom. "Where is it? What did you do with it?"

He let up the pressure of the knife so she could answer.

Her mind reeled. "I don't know what you're talking about."

"You don't know?" He pushed the knife against her neck again.

She shook her head. "I have no idea."

"Don't play coy with me. There are two of you. One of you will tell me where it is."

She dared not cry out, fearing that he might slice the knife across her throat and seek the information he needed from Mel. Mr. Knife had made it clear he wasn't opposed to killing her.

Still gripping her upper arm, he pulled the knife away from her throat, twisted her around and pushed her against the wall. He shoved an arm underneath her chin and pressed up. Her neck muscles strained, and she struggled for breath.

His eyes looked almost yellow. His breath stank like rotten eggs. Even in the dim light, she'd gotten a good look at him.

"That was our payday you took."

She shook her head. "No, I didn't take anything." He'd used the word *our*. Was there another killer stalking through this house? Mel had said as much.

"Liar." He took the pressure off her neck but pushed her to one side. Her chest slammed against a commercial popcorn machine.

She righted herself and prepared to fight back. The knife still glinted in his hand. Pushing the popcorn machine on its casters, she created a barrier between them and backed him into a corner. She took the opportunity to run from him past four rows of movie-theater chairs down toward a movie screen. The floor was raked just like in a theater.

There was no door by the screen. No way to escape. She hurried around it toward the door beyond the far aisle.

Mr. Knife raced after her, grabbing her shirt just as she reached for the doorknob. She turned and kicked him in the leg. He yelped in pain. Isabel flung the door open and found herself running down a long dark hallway. Straining to see clearly, she turned a corner and peered out a window. No footsteps came toward her. She must have shaken Mr. Knife or he'd taken a wrong turn.

She slid it open and climbed out into the cold. Snow swirled around her and the wind nearly knocked her over. With the pending darkness and blizzard, she could see maybe three or four feet in front of her. Grateful for Mel's coat, she shoved her hands in the warm pockets.

When she looked behind her, the wind was blowing enough to cover her tracks. Victoria Wilson's art studio was out here somewhere. Though she'd never had reason to go inside it, she'd seen it from the house.

The snow pelted her and she forged ahead until an A-frame structure came into view.

Finding the door unlocked, she pushed inside and fell on the floor, out of breath.

Isabel shut the door and pushed a large metal sculpture against it.

In addition to the artist's supplies, the studio had a couch and a woodstove. She dared not start a fire. It might be spotted from the house. She gathered the blanket off the couch and wrapped it around her.

The sky was already growing dark. Was she going to die out here? Today was her day off and no one but Mel and the Wilsons knew she was up here. But she still wasn't sure she could trust Mel, and the Wilsons wouldn't know to worry about her until it was too late.

Isabel buried her face in her hands. What a mess.

She shook her head. "Izzy, you seem to have a gift for getting into messes."

Her mother had always said that she wouldn't amount to anything. Maybe Mom was right. Even when she was trying to do the right thing by being conscientious about her work, it seemed to end in disaster.

She wrapped the blanket tighter around her and the melody of a hymn came into her head. She hummed it and then sang the words. She calmed a little.

God was her refuge and she could rest beneath His wing. She closed her eyes tight. She had to believe that. Somehow this would all work out.

The door rattled and she jumped. A fist pounded on the thick wood.

"Isabel, it's me."

That was Mel's voice.

She hesitated. Did she really want to let him in? She still didn't know how he was connected to all this chaos. He seemed interested in keeping her safe, but his secrecy bothered her.

The pounding stopped. A moment later his face appeared at the window by the couch. He tapped on the glass.

She had a decision to make. Did she trust him or not?

Jason stamped his feet to stave off the cold. When he'd gone to search for Isabel in the house and couldn't find her, he remembered her talking about the art studio that was separate from the main house.

Was she really not going to let him in? He couldn't stay out here in the cold much longer. Though he'd grabbed a jacket he found hung on a hook, the chill had sunk down into his bones and his fingers were numbed.

He heard a scraping noise. She was moving something across the floor.

"Come inside." Isabel sounded out of breath.

He hurried around the little building and mounted three steps to open the door. The room was full of metal, canvases and easels. Isabel had retreated to the far corner by a couch, a blanket wrapped around her shoulders.

"Are you cold?" She stepped across the room and pushed the heavy metal object back against the door.

He nodded. She'd hesitated but she'd let him in. Maybe she was starting to understand that he wasn't the bad guy.

She pointed toward the end of the couch. "There's a blanket over there."

He pulled back the curtain on the only window. Though the artist studio was only partially hidden by a grove of trees, he saw no sign that their pursuer had figured out where they'd gone.

He gathered the blanket around his shoulders. Silence descended and coiled around the room. With the blanket still wrapped around his shoulders, he rose from the couch and paced.

"I take it your phone still doesn't work?"

He shook his head. "The storm must be wreaking havoc with the signal." His eyes rested on a bowl full of wrapped mini candy bars. He picked it up and walked toward Isabel, who took several out of the bowl and whispered a thank-you. She gazed at him with big round doe eyes.

Though most of the time she was so guarded, she had a softness to her that he felt drawn to.

"Mrs. Wilson must eat these while she's waiting to be inspired, huh?" He grabbed a few pieces for himself before setting the bowl back down.

The remark brought only a faint smile to Isabel's face. "I don't know that much about her personal habits." She rose to her feet. "She's got a sink over here to rinse her brushes out. Do you want some water?"

"Sure."

The faucet sputtered and spit while Isabel filled two paper cups, but at least it wasn't frozen. She handed him one of the cups and then sat back down.

The cool liquid soothed his dry throat.

Jason let the blanket fall to the floor while he paced. She really did act like she worked for a property management company just as she'd said when she'd first opened the door to him. It was clear to him now that she was an innocent in all this mess.

"That man who chased us. He wants something. He thinks I have it." She lifted her head and narrowed her eyes. "What's going on here?"

A debate raged in his head. How much should he tell her? So the thief was trying to find the bookmark. That meant it must have been moved. Only one person could have moved it.

They were trapped here until the storm broke. Taking the bookmark would reinforce the ruse that they wanted to be part of the smuggling ring. "Part of your job must be to tidy up before owners of the house come to stay."

"A little bit. Sometimes workers have left a mess in the owner's absence or things just look out of place." She shrugged. "That sort of thing."

Her eyes held a certain serenity, a total lack of guile. He wondered how much of his hand he should show. "Do you think you might have moved the thing the thief was looking for?"

She thought about it. "Nothing of value." She shook her head. "Besides, if he wants to steal things there is plenty of expensive stuff to take in that house."

"It sounds like he's looking for one thing in particular."

"It sounds like you know more than you're telling me, Mel." Her voice held a bit of an edge. "Like exactly what he's looking for."

His initial impression of her had been that she was soft and refined. But something in those eyes told him she had a spine of steel underneath. He admired that about her.

He let out a breath. "My name isn't Mel. It's

Jason. I got that shirt at a thrift store. It's useful in my line of work."

"So, you lied about your name." She continued to study him, waiting for a deeper explanation. "What is your line of work?"

How much did he dare tell her? Chances were the bookmark was in some container that looked like junk but that the pickup man would recognize as his package. "So this thing that man is looking for. Do you think you may have been tidying up and moved it?"

"Why are you after the same thing they are, Jason?" Suspicion colored her words.

"He's not leaving until he gets what he came here for. Maybe we can find it." In order to keep the investigation under wraps, he needed to continue the fiction that he and Isabel were thieves who wanted in on the smuggling ring. Getting that bookmark might open the door to going undercover and infiltrating the smuggling ring, as long as he could get Isabel out of danger.

"And do what—give it to him? He disabled both our cars. I don't think he wants us to leave here alive. He thinks you and I are after the same thing he is." She looked right at him. "I don't like being accused of being a thief."

Her words filled with intensity. He didn't want her involved in this. Once they were out of here—if they got out of here—maybe he could get her some protection. "I wish I could tell you more, but I can't."

"I don't even know what that man—or men, if there is another guy—came here for. But you do, don't you?"

He studied her for a long moment. Her stare made him feel like she could see beneath his skin. She was shrewd.

A hundred contradictory impulses charged through his head at once. The thieves thought he and Isabel were trying to horn in on their territory. Getting that bookmark would help the Bureau with their investigation and give him that much more cred with them, but he also had to find a way to get Isabel safely disentangled from this mess.

Private detective work could be feast or famine. The FBI throwing him a job from time to time would help keep the wolves from the door.

One thing was clear. Isabel was smart enough to play tit for tat. She wasn't going to give him any information until he gave her some. "I'm a private detective. Yesterday, a man dropped off a gold bookmark at this house. It's worth a great deal of money. The two men in the house were supposed to pick it up. You weren't supposed to be here. No one was." The less she knew, the better. Best not tell her about the FBI or the scope of the smuggling ring.

Her posture softened a little. Maybe she was warming up to him. "The people who own the house had a change of plans. They're coming earlier than expected. I'm the only one who knew that."

She rose to her feet and faced him, letting the blanket fall to the ground. "So what are we going to do? We could wait the night out here. They probably don't know about this studio."

"They might start searching the property once they can't find us in the house," he said. "I'm thinking it's not just one guy either. He has a partner."

She pressed her lips together. "Yes, I think you're right about that." She started to pace. "I believe the one with the knife won't hesitate to use it." She shivered and wrapped her arms around herself. "We really need the police."

"It would be better if we didn't get the police involved. I can't say why. Besides, I'm pretty sure they wouldn't be able to get up that road until the storm stops and it's plowed." Making an arrest at this point in the investigation might tip the head of the smuggling ring off.

She flopped down on the couch and stared at a blank canvas across the room. Then she studied him again. Her cheeks were flushed with color and he liked the way her blond curls framed her face. He didn't like the suspicion he saw in her eyes, though.

Finally, she bent her head. She put her feet one on top of the other, then switched the bottom one to the top. "I've made a mess of everything. I'll probably lose my job. Trouble just seems to find me no matter how hard I try to do the right thing."

Picking up on the deep pain in her voice, he sat down on the opposite end of the couch. "None of this is your fault."

She laced her fingers together and then drew them apart over and over. "The Wilsons are expecting to come home to a cozy warm house."

It would be better for the operation if the homeowners didn't find the house in disarray. But they would probably just assume it was a run-of-the-mill break-in. He wasn't sure why she was fixated on doing her job considering a man with a knife was stalking them. "Look, the thieves are searching for that bookmark."

She lifted her head and stared at him as fear filled her voice. "Don't you think staying safe should be our priority?"

"We're not safe as long as they are here. Finding it could give us some leverage."

She wasn't totally buying his story. He had to hand it to her—she was pretty savvy at reading him.

"Chances are, it was in some kind of container. Did you throw things away? Did you move them around?"

"Of course I did. I hurried through the house and straightened up a bunch of stuff and then you knocked on the door. I don't remember every little item. I did throw some things away in the kitchen. I suppose we could check the garbage."

"That would be a start," he said. They still had to find a way out of here. "I didn't notice any cars other than yours or mine. Is there anything parked in that garage?"

She stood up and walked toward him shaking her head. "The Wilsons bring their own car."

Jason's thoughts raced as he tried to come up with a plan. "The thief must have parked his car a ways from the property." That meant even if the thieves wanted to leave, they probably couldn't until the storm let up. They wouldn't risk freezing in the blizzard. Jason and Isabel were trapped here and so were the two thieves.

What would be the best thing to do? To wait it out and hope they wouldn't be found here… or to go back to the house? One thing was certain: they needed to stay together.

He stood up and looked out the window.

Night would be falling soon. They'd have the cover of darkness. It wasn't that long a walk from the studio to the house, but in blizzard conditions, it would be easy enough to get disoriented.

As a boy, he remembered his father, a sheriff in another county, telling stories of men who froze to death walking from a barn to the house in whiteout conditions.

Isabel shifted a little closer to him. "We don't know anything about the other guy. What if he has a gun?"

Jason had thought of that too. "When are the Wilsons supposed to get here?"

"Tomorrow afternoon. I have other houses to deal with tomorrow, so I had to fit this one in today."

The door rattled and shook. Jason took a step back. It could have been the wind.

"It's really blowing out there." Isabel's voice held only a trace of fear. "I say we stay here."

He nodded and then looked around the studio space for anything that might be of use.

His search was interrupted by the glass in the window shattering.

FOUR

A scream caught in Isabel's throat. Glass flew everywhere as a gun was fired through the window. Both of them ducked to the floor. She lifted her head. Though she could only discern his silhouette, this was a different man than Mr. Knife, shorter and more muscular.

Jason grabbed her and led her toward the door, where he pushed away the heavy metal sculpture.

Mr. Gun must know they'd try the door.

Her gaze darted around the room. There was no other way to escape.

Jason yanked open the door and drew his own gun. They rushed out into the dark of night. The cold permeated her skin almost immediately. Wind pushed on her body. Swordlike snowflakes sliced across her face and neck.

Jason's hand slipped into hers. She bent her head to shield it from the assault of the storm.

Gunfire reverberated through the woods. Any

doubt that Mr. Knife had an accomplice was removed. Mr. Gun was after them.

Jason's fingers gripped hers like iron. He pulled her sideways until they entered a grove of trees that provided only a small amount of shelter.

Through the haze of snow, she saw a light bob past them. Jason aimed his gun toward the light but didn't pull the trigger. Once it was clear their pursuer hadn't seen them, he put the gun back in his waistband.

Mr. Gun was probably better dressed and equipped to deal with the snow, and he had a flashlight.

Isabel shivered. If she was cold, Jason must be close to hypothermia with thin layers of fabric to protect him.

He leaned close to her and whispered in her ear. "He's gone past us."

He took her hand again, which warmed hers despite the conditions. He wove through the trees.

"Do you know where you're going?"

"I'm hoping to see light from the house," he said.

The sheets of snow and darkness made it hard to see the landscape clearly. "There was no light on in the house earlier. I think the storm might have knocked out the electricity."

As they stumbled through the trees, she felt hope fading. One small light that pierced the reduced visibility of the storm was all they needed.

"He went ahead of us. Watch for his flashlight," Jason said. He had to lean close to her and shout to be heard above the shrill cry of the storm.

She could barely see three feet in front of her. They would have to be right on top of the thief before they saw him. It was a dangerous game they were playing.

Jason claimed he was not on the wrong side of the law. His story made sense…sort of. Why he needed the bookmark was a little perplexing. Even if he was a detective, maybe he saw the possibility of financial gain in finding it. It wouldn't be the first time a law-enforcement guy was on the take.

She leaned closer to him and trudged forward. Not because she totally trusted him, but because getting too far away from him increased her chances of ending up a Popsicle.

Up ahead, a light winked in and out of view. They veered toward where they'd last seen it.

Wind pressed on her from three sides like being inside a vacuum cleaner. Its howling and the creaking of trees surrounded her. She lifted her head slightly, hoping to see the light again.

Isabel squinted against the onslaught of icy snow and intense wind. The pinpricks of the flakes on her skin were like a thousand tiny needles.

Jason wrapped an arm around her waist and pulled her in a new direction. He must have seen something she'd missed. If they got too close to the thief, he would shoot them.

She lifted her head again, thinking the house should've come into view by now. Jason let go of her. She reached out for his hand as her heart squeezed tight with fear. He was her lifeline. She did not want to get lost in this storm.

He caught her hand again.

The house appeared suddenly in her field of vision. They were only feet away from it. Jason pulled her toward him. She reached out for the security of the outside wall.

When they got the door open, they both fell inside onto a tiled floor.

Before she even had time to take a deep breath—now that she wasn't fighting wind, snow and cold—she heard footsteps pounding, growing louder. The room was almost completely dark.

Jason tugged on her sleeve. He opened a

small door, and they both crawled inside. The space was so small they sat facing each other, knees touching. They seemed to be in some sort of laundry chute.

Footsteps seemed to be pounding all around them. Had Mr. Knife figured out they were in the house or was his frantic search for something else? The footsteps grew closer. Maybe Mr. Gun was in the house by now.

Isabel could hear the sound of her own breathing in the tiny space.

The footsteps stopped.

Jason whispered only one word. "Down."

She angled her body and slid down the aluminum slide, landing on a pile of linens.

Jason's silhouette blotted out some of the bright light that shone from the top of the chute from the thieves' flashlight. Jason slid down beside her on the pile of dirty laundry.

She was grateful the cleaning crew hadn't tossed the sheets in the washing machine like they were supposed to.

Jason squeezed her elbow. "Come on. He's going to find this room soon enough."

She glanced back up the chute, which had gone dark. Apparently, Mr. Knife, or maybe it was Mr. Gun, had opted not to follow them down it, which meant he was using the stairs.

She leaped to her feet, falling in behind him and squinting to see in the dark room.

"There has to be a good place to hide," said Jason.

Though she had been through the ten-thousand-square-foot home many times, she hadn't been thinking about hiding places. Even as Jason started moving toward the door, she racked her brain.

They hurried down a hallway.

She tugged on his arm. "He'll be coming down the stairs. We can't go that way."

"I know, but he'll be looking for us on this floor."

She turned and ran in the other direction. There had to be another way up to the main floor. They ran past the laundry room. Footsteps sounded above them. She sprinted toward a door and swung it open, finding a narrow back stairway similar to servants' stairs in older houses. These stairs led into the kitchen. Probably so cooks had quick, discreet access to any food and wine stored in the basement.

The stairs were not carpeted, which made the potential for noise that much greater. Stepping as softly as possible, they hurried up and into the kitchen. There was no place to hide in the kitchen that wouldn't be obvious. Isabel grabbed keys off a hook where they were hanging. She filed through them, holding them close to her face to see better.

She'd never been in the greenhouse but had noticed the labeled key for it. Maybe they could lock it from the inside. Jason leaned close to her, trying to see what she was doing. She could feel his warm breath on her neck.

A pang of guilt shot through her. She wasn't supposed to go into the greenhouse. That wasn't part of her job. She vowed that if she got a chance, she'd explain and apologize to the Wilsons. If she got the chance…

Isabel felt along the wall for the door that led to the greenhouse where it connected with the kitchen. She leaned close to the keyhole in an effort to insert the key. Humid air floated around her when she opened the door.

They slipped inside. The room was filled with plants though she could not discern what kind in the dim light. The Wilsons must hire a gardener to care for the plants in their absence.

The door did not lock from the inside.

Through the clear glass, a shadow stalked past them.

Jason pulled Isabel to the floor. Her heart revved into high gear as they scurried around to the far side of a bench and slipped into a tight space between the tall potting benches. At least they were out of view. Once again, their knees were touching as they faced each other in a small space.

After a moment, Jason spoke in a hushed tone. "Can you remember what you straightened up and what you threw away?"

Isabel waited for her heart to slow down before responding. Of course he was thinking about the bookmark. She closed her eyes, trying to remember. "There were some things left in the kitchen by the cleaning crew, just packaging from cleaning products."

"No boxes or anything that something might be hidden in."

Her memory fogged. The whole thing felt like it had happened a lifetime ago. "I'm not sure. I just automatically straighten up as I do my first walk through the house."

"It's okay." He reached over and touched her knee. "I know this violence is probably not what you're used to."

He had no idea. She'd pulled off her impression of respectability enough that he probably would never guess that running from the law, sneaking around and hiding were what she was proficient in at one time in her life.

"Can you visualize the rooms you went into and what you did in each one?"

She understood what he was doing. They couldn't just randomly go banging through the house. They had to be stealthy about where they searched.

She closed her eyes and tried to remember. Her usual routine was to go to the kitchen first and throw out food in the cupboards that looked like it was past its expiration date and then walk through the main rooms in the house, but was that what she had done this time? "Mostly I just closed doors and straightened things."

She lifted her head in time to see a bright light flashing. "He's coming this way."

Both of them rolled underneath benches that held heavy foliage.

The door creaked open. Footsteps tapped on the concrete floor as the flashlight illuminated different sections of the room.

Isabel held her breath. Her stomach pressed against the cold concrete floor. The thief leaned over and shone the light beneath the benches, coming within a few inches of where she hid.

Oh God, don't let him find us.

The thief dropped the flashlight. It rolled across the floor, lighting up the area just in front of Jason's face.

The flashlight blinked on and off. The batteries must've been failing. The thief picked it up and tapped it on his palm. The light stabilized for a moment and then went out altogether.

The thief cursed.

She heard a second voice at the doorway. "Come on. We got to hurry."

"My flashlight went out, man." The voice was Mr. Knife's.

"Never mind. I have mine. Forget about those two for now. Let's keep looking. We got to get out of here as soon as there is a break in the storm."

"What if they have it already?"

After a long pause, Mr. Gun spoke up. "We'll find them soon enough and deal with them whether they have the merchandise or not."

Mr. Knife let out a heavy breath that sounded more like a groan. "Yeah, they'll get what's coming to them. No one horns in on our sweet deal."

The words chilled Isabel to the bone. She remained still until she could no longer hear their footsteps. Jason had already rolled out from underneath the bench.

Her eyes had adjusted more to the darkness, and she could see actual plants, vegetables and orchids instead of just shadows and outlines. Her eyes landed on a book placed on a waist-high bench, probably a book about gardening. Why else would it be in here?

A memory clicked in her head. Books...out of place. "I picked up some books that were by the entryway table and put them back in the library on the fourth floor." When she'd first arrived, she'd whirred through the house picking up, throwing away and straightening.

"That would be a good place to hide a bookmark," he said. "Lead the way."

They'd have to go through the house and take the main stairway to get to it.

As though he'd read her mind, Jason said, "Maybe I should lead the way."

"Good idea."

"Stay low and close to the wall," he said.

They slipped out of the greenhouse and into the shadows. Isabel pressed close to Jason and listened for the sound of approaching assassins.

Jason scanned the open area on the main floor and then searched the darker corners for movement. He hated putting Isabel at risk like this, but the last time he'd left her alone, the man with the knife had taken her. The safest place for her in a house with armed men bent on killing them was right by his side.

It made sense that the bookmark was in some books on the entryway table. Hiding things in plain sight was the strategy of the courier who dropped off the stolen treasure.

Jason had taken footage through a window of a painting stolen from a European art gallery. The drop-off man had hung it among the much more amateur efforts of the homeowner. This information helped the FBI understand the mind of the man or woman who was engineering the smuggling. There had to be easier ways to smuggle valuables into the country. There must be a reason why the mastermind chose vacation homes.

The whole investigation was quite involved. Several other private investigators had been hired to watch unoccupied houses for activity. Usually, the Bureau would get wind of items being stolen in different parts of the world from US Customs or foreign governments, and then within a week or so, activity would pick up in Silver Strike.

Jason and Isabel hurried toward the stairs with Isabel taking the lead since she knew the layout of the house.

Light flashed at the end of the hallway.

Jason pressed against the wall and held out a protective hand toward Isabel. She stood close enough for her soft hair to brush under his chin. Her hand cupped his arm just above the elbow. Her touch sent a charge of electricity through him.

She was afraid, but brave enough to keep her cool.

The light disappeared into a room.

Isabel tugged on Jason's sleeve and turned to take the stairs that led to the second floor.

The thieves had to know the bookmark was in a book. They must have found the library by now but clearly hadn't found the bookmark. He hoped they weren't walking into a trap.

He glanced over his shoulder. The light bobbed at the end of the hallway but didn't reach them.

They raced up to the second-story landing, which was almost completely dark. They had only a short stairway to get up to the dome.

The pounding of footfalls behind them reached Jason's ear. Then the cool metal of a knife blade pressed into his neck. He steeled himself against the attack, ready to fight back.

"Go," he said to the darkness, hoping that Isabel would understand.

He could handle this guy but he didn't want her hurt.

"Where is it?" said the thief. "We looked in the library."

Jason elbowed the man in the stomach. The man backed away. In the darkness, Jason had to rely on his other senses to figure out where his opponent was. He was grateful for the years he'd spent studying martial arts.

He swung at the air, colliding with flesh. A

hand gripped his wrist and yanked him around. His head rammed against a wall. Stunned, he whirled around and landed a blow that made the man groan. He hit the man's back with a karate chop. The thief fell to the floor, making a cracking sound followed by another thud.

Jason braced himself for the man to jump to his feet and lay into him again, but he didn't move. Jason kicked him. He must have hit his head against the banister. Jason leaned over. The man was still breathing but out cold.

He felt around for the knife but couldn't find it, and he couldn't waste any more time. The noise of the fight might have alerted the other man on the floor below and that guy had a flashlight and a gun.

Jason hurried down the hallway in the direction he'd heard Isabel's footsteps retreating. When he felt for his phone in his shirt pocket it was gone. It must have fallen out in the fight. There was no time to search for it now. He reached out a hand to the textured wall to orient himself. Up ahead he saw light.

The whiteness of the overcast sky provided some illumination through the glass dome of the library. It looked like the storm was letting up. Isabel was pulling books off the shelf and flipping through them. A stack already sat on the floor that she or the thieves had worked through.

She turned toward him. "Quick—lock the door."

He shut the door and turned the latch.

"You don't remember which book?"

"I know I put them away in this area here." She swept her hand across a section of shelves.

"Any sign that the thieves were here?"

She pointed across the room. The library was round with books that ran from the floor to the edge of the glass dome. "Those books over there are arranged by size and color. Don't ask. It's a rich-people thing." She grabbed another book off the shelf and filed through it. "Anyway, they are out of place. Those guys must have gone through those books searching. I got to hand it to them. They are tidy."

Maybe the thieves wouldn't get as big a payday if there was any evidence of a break-in. During the other jobs, the thieves had used lock picks or had known the security codes and nothing had been disturbed.

With a backward glance at the door, Jason grabbed a book and riffled through it. "Is there another way out of here in case we have to make a speedy exit?"

She pointed to a door. "It leads to another

balcony. This one has stairs. No way could we drop four floors and live."

He grabbed another book and leafed through it. If he lifted it toward the dome, he could see better. He put the volume back in place and grabbed another. At best, they had minutes before the thief on the floor below came to and headed toward them.

Isabel pulled books and flipped through them at a furious pace.

Someone banged on the door and wiggled the handle.

Jason worked even faster. "It's got to be here somewhere."

The pounding stopped. Jason moved closer to the door and listened. "He's picking the lock." He stalked back to the bookshelf and pulled another hardback.

Isabel slid a book back into place and grabbed another. She bent the spine of the hardback. A shiny object fell to the floor. She picked it up.

"Jason," she said. She had found it.

"Let's go," he said. She shoved the bookmark in the pocket of the coat he'd given her and zipped it.

The door burst open as they raced toward the balcony. The short muscular man raised his gun and fired off a shot. Isabel grabbed Jason's hand.

Jason pushed open the door that led to the balcony.

They descended with the armed man at their heels. Another shot blasted through the silent night but it went wide. Even with the flashlight, the man couldn't see much better than they could.

Jason could hear the footfalls behind him. They had to find a way to shake this guy and find a hiding place. Isabel held tight to his hand. She understood the importance of not getting separated.

He stayed close to the house, running the full length of it. They ended up in the driveway beside his useless van. He crouched low and Isabel slipped in beside him. Footsteps pounded past and then faded.

"He might come back," she whispered.

Jason hurried to the side of the van and eased the passenger door open. "Get in. I suspect he'll go in the house to get his accomplice first."

She complied.

"Crawl toward the back and stay low."

He got in behind her. His surveillance equipment was stacked in a corner though barely visible in the near darkness.

"How long do you think we should stay here?" Isabel kept her voice to a whisper.

"Not long." He rifled around in the dark, taking the time to lock each door. "I have another coat in here, extra hat and gloves." He slipped into the heavier coat and tossed the gloves and hat toward Isabel.

He dug through another pile of stuff to find a hat and pair of gloves for himself. It wasn't his first day at camp. He always had lots of cold-weather gear on hand.

He grabbed his keys out of the ignition. The key ring had a small flashlight on it that might be useful.

He pulled the gun out from his waistband and stared at it. Though he went to the range every week, he had never had to use the gun while working. It might come down to that tonight.

Jason could not see Isabel's expression in the darkness, but he sensed the tension that had invaded the tiny space.

"Detectives carry guns. That's just how it is." He held out his hand. "Can I see the bookmark?"

Suspicion clouded her voice. "Why?"

Jason's stomach coiled into a tight knot. Here they were, back at square one again. If she didn't trust him, they might not survive the night. They had to work together. Both their lives depended on it.

Why was it so hard to win her trust?

FIVE

Isabel looked at what appeared to be a computer screen and keyboard. "What is all this stuff? Surveillance equipment?" So far, Jason had done nothing to harm her and had risked his own safety to help her. Maybe he really was a detective. That didn't mean he was an honest detective. Past experience told her not to be too quick to trust. Jason was keeping secrets, and she didn't like that. What was he hiding? She touched the pocket where she'd placed the bookmark.

Jason let out a heavy breath and shook his head. "Hold on to the bookmark if you want."

Her chest squeezed tight with indecision. "I don't like liars." The intensity of her words surprised her. The pain of what she had been through with Nick was still very close to the surface despite how long it had been—she still had not let any man into her life or heart. But she had started to think Jason might be okay.

That scared her. How had he managed find the chink in her armor in such a short time? So what if he was protective and kept her safe. He was still a man and men always let you down in the end.

"I don't like liars either, Isabel, but if I tell you what is going on, it puts you at greater risk."

Jason's voice had a soothing quality, not the anger or impatience she would have expected. She laced her fingers together and clenched her jaw.

Don't be taken in.

He turned from side to side, searching. "At least put some cardboard around it. If it gets damaged, it loses its value."

"Maybe you are a detective, but I think you are on the take." Her accusation lacked conviction. She could feel her resolve to not trust him weakening in the face of his gentle response.

He tore a section of cardboard off an empty box. "Give me the bookmark. I promise to give it back to you if that's what you want."

She unzipped the coat and slipped her hand into the inside pocket.

"I promise," he repeated.

How many times had she heard that?

She grasped the bookmark and handed it to him. Their fingers touched briefly. He placed it carefully in the folded cardboard. She tensed, waiting for the moment when he'd shove it in his pocket and pull the gun on her.

He held it out for her to take.

She let out a breath. "Keep it." So he'd kept one small promise. He still had a lot of explaining to do.

A light flashed outside.

"He's coming this way."

The light had shone through the windshield. Jason touched her arm. "Out the back. Hurry."

He pushed open the van doors. They bolted toward the house, pressing against the brick walls. The eaves of the roof provided even more darkness to hide in as footsteps pounded around the van and drew closer.

Jason pushed on Isabel's shoulder, indicating she should keep moving. The cold seeped into her face as she made her way along the outside wall. They needed to find a good hiding place.

Isabel thought about the layout of the house. The wine cellar in the basement had a stairway leading up to the outside. They wouldn't be trapped if they hid there and needed to make a run for it.

"This way." She tugged on the sleeve of his coat and led him around to a side entrance.

Isabel pressed her hand against the exposed brick and struggled to get her bearings in the dark house as they moved down a set of stairs.

Footsteps pounded on the floor above them. They'd lost their pursuer for now.

Her heart raced as she felt along the wall, waiting for her eyes to adjust to the darkness. She pushed open a door. The shelves of wine were barely discernible.

Jason slipped in beside her. His shoulder pressed against hers. A tense silence fell around them, interrupted by footsteps above them that came in short bursts.

"They're still looking," she whispered.

"It's just a matter of time. We have to find a way to get out of here. They have a car parked somewhere close by."

"We could freeze trying to find it."

"We need a sure thing. Aren't there any neighbors close by?"

Isabel shook her head. "The nearest one might be miles away. They are up the road, not down. This is the first house in the subdivision." Though the storm had let up, it was still dark and cold out there. She squeezed her eyes shut, mulling over what Jason had said. A sure thing. There were no other vehicles on the property or houses close by, but... "There's a communal building. That is one of the perks of this subdivision."

"This is a subdivision?"

"Yes, but the houses are miles apart."

"What's in the building?"

"I've only seen it on a map. But it's like a clubhouse where you can have get-togethers, and there's a building with snowmobiles and ATVs. My boss explained to me what the building was used for."

"How far is it from here?"

"I'd estimate less than a mile. We can use the trees for cover but we'll get lost if we don't keep the road in sight." In these conditions, she'd be guessing at the location of the building.

His voice dropped half an octave. "That's a long way to go in the cold."

Footsteps pounded down the stairs. Both of them pressed deeper into the shadows. The footsteps drew closer. Doors opened and shut. The thief was searching all of the rooms in the basement, making his way down the hallway. Isabel's heart beat so loudly she feared it would give them away.

They had only seconds to make a decision. "We stay here, they will find and kill us." His hand slipped into hers as he led the way up the stairs to the door that took them back out into the cold night.

A blast of cold air hit her face, causing her cheeks to tingle. His gloved hand gripped hers.

"Which way?"

She pointed as the chill settled on her exposed

skin. He ran toward the trees. She held on to his hand. When she glanced over her shoulder, she saw light glowing in the dome and a silhouetted figure.

By the door through which they'd just exited a light also bobbed. It loomed toward them for some time and then stopped. Would they give up the chase that easily? Somehow, she doubted it.

The trees grew thicker as the outline of the house disappeared. She focused on the sound of her feet padding on the soft snow. Her breath came out in vapory puffs as she struggled to keep pace with Jason.

Doubt plagued her every footstep. Would they be able to get into the clubhouse garage? She wasn't sure they'd even find the place in the dark.

She heard the sound of a motor, a car on the road.

The clang of an engine revving up landed on her ears. Headlights cut through the trees behind her. The thieves had gone back for their car. She quickened her pace. Jason grabbed her and pulled her into the trees as the thieves' car drew near.

Heart shifting into high gear, Jason climbed uphill through the trees to get off the road. Isabel remained close beside him.

The car motor grew louder, more menacing. The headlights flashed by them and then the motor settled into an idle. Voices were raised, commands shouted. A car door slammed and then the car eased down the road. One man must have gotten out to search on foot while the other moved past them.

Out of breath, Jason kept pushing uphill. He craned his neck, catching just a flash of light through the thick trees.

Isabel caught up to him. She spoke between deep breaths. They both kept climbing. "They must have seen us on the road."

Jason glanced around, not able to discern much of anything. They needed a hiding place, time to catch their breath. How were they going to find the clubhouse if they couldn't navigate by the road?

The car rolled by again on the road. This time headed in the direction of the house.

Jason sprinted faster, though his legs were screaming from the effort of moving uphill. The man on foot with the flashlight was still at the bottom of the hill, looking up in their direction.

Jason ran up to a large evergreen, gesturing toward Isabel and speaking in a whisper. "Scoot down toward the trunk. The boughs will hide us."

She complied with his order. He crawled in

beside her. Both of them were out of breath. The tree sheltered them from the wind and snow.

"We need to get back down to the road," she leaned close and whispered. Her breath warmed his ear.

He nodded.

Branches creaked around them in the wind. Down below, the car continued to go back and forth on the road. He could not see the headlights anymore but heard the engine grow louder and then dim.

A distinctly human grunt emanated below them. A tree branch cracked, probably the searcher stepping on deadfall. Footsteps seemed to surround them. Isabel pressed closer to him. He could see nothing through the darkness and thick foliage.

The footsteps seemed to fade and then grow louder. He couldn't hear the car engine any longer. Had the driver decided to search farther down the road?

His breathing slowed. They huddled in the darkness…waiting. He heard noises that were most likely human.

Isabel had pulled her knees up to her chest and wrapped her arms around them. Her head was tilted. After several minutes of silence in the forest, she spoke up. "Do you think he's gone?"

Five, maybe ten, minutes had passed since

Hidden Away

he'd heard any sound that might have come from their pursuers.

"Stay put." He crawled on all fours to get out from under the tree, then remained crouching, listening and watching. Though it was still snowing, the wind had died down.

He signaled for Isabel to come out. When she was close, he whispered, "We'll walk parallel to the road but use the trees for cover. Until we can find a safe spot to emerge."

She nodded as he rose and walked in a serpentine pattern through the trees. Always, his ears tuned for any out-of-place sound. Isabel stayed close to him.

The trees thinned, and he could see the road below. The thieves must have a pretty heavy-duty vehicle to be driving on the unplowed roads. At least five or six inches must have fallen since the start of the storm. Enough moonlight shone through to give the snow the appearance of being garnished with diamonds.

The quiet was deceptive. He knew he needed to stay on his guard. The two thieves were close, even if he couldn't hear or see them. Every step they took brought them closer to danger.

SIX

Isabel tried to ignore the tight knot in her stomach by focusing on the back of Jason's head. In the darkness, she could just make out the band of white on his knit hat. She took in an intense breath and looked side to side. They could be walking right into the thieves' path.

She heard a noise to the side of her. Jason kept walking. She reached for the hem of his coat. Then she saw the glint of light up the hill. He wrapped his arms around her and guided her behind one of the larger trees.

Her heart thudded in her ears. As they faced each other, she tilted her head and looked up at Jason, whose posture indicated he was still on high alert. He turned and angled around the tree, then looked back at her and lifted his chin, indicating they should keep moving.

He worked his way down toward more level ground and spurred himself into a jog. It would be hard to find the clubhouse, a place she'd

never been to. What if they overshot it altogether? They could be wandering for hours.
The cold was as much an enemy as the two
thieves.

The trees thinned and the ground became
more level.

Jason slowed so she could catch up. "We must
be getting close."

The evergreens were so far apart they didn't
provide any cover. They made their way toward
the road. Tracks indicated that the thieves' car
had come this far.

She stopped to scan the trees behind her, seeing nothing.

Jason picked up the pace. She sprinted beside him as a sense of urgency pressed in on her
from all sides. Now they were out in the open,
exposed. They needed to hurry. The tracks left
by the car ended where the thief had turned
around. A good sign that the men weren't waiting to ambush them at the clubhouse.

Up ahead she spotted a cluster of trees and
the faint outline of what might be a building.
Jason veered in that direction. She sprinted to
keep up with him, scanning their surroundings.

Gradually two buildings came into view. Picnic tables outside were covered in snow. The
clubhouse was about fifty yards from the road.

Isabel quickened her pace as she prayed they'd be able to access the snowmobiles. She ran ahead of Jason but slowed as she got close to the garage. There was a padlock on the door. She shook the doorknob out of frustration as her hope vaporized.

"Now what are we going to do?" Her eyes warmed with tears.

Jason peered into a window. "We made it this far. There has to be a solution."

She ran toward the clubhouse door. It too was locked. Even if there was a landline in there, it might not be working. She hung her head, squeezed her eyes tight to keep the tears from coming.

Come on, Izzy. You've been in worse situations. Be strong.

Jason squeezed her upper arm. His voice filled with compassion. "We'll figure something out. If I had something like a paper clip, I could pick the lock. Split up. Let's keep looking for a way in." He took off in one direction and she ran around the side of the clubhouse. The windows of the clubhouse were high and small, but maybe they could climb in.

"Isabel." Jason's voice came from behind the garage.

She ran along the garage wall to the back,

where Jason was sweeping the snow off an ATV with a plow on it.

"Your chariot awaits." His voice was almost jovial.

"Someone must have left it out here because they knew they'd be plowing again."

"There's no key," he said as he dug into his pockets. He handed her a set of keys. "There's a tiny flashlight on there."

Isabel shone the light where Jason pointed.

On the road on the other side of the garage, a car rumbled. Isabel's heart squeezed tight. It had to be the thieves. No one else would be out on a night like tonight.

"Give me the light. I can kinda see if I put it on the seat." Jason's focus never wavered from the ATV. "Check to make sure it's them. It might be the guy coming back for his plow."

Jason's optimism didn't make much sense to her. All the same, she ran to the edge of the building and peered around the side of it. A car was parked on the road. A man had gotten out and was making his way in the deep snow toward the clubhouse. Though it was hard to see any detail, he was built like the short muscular man she'd encountered at the Wilsons' house.

She hurried back to where Jason was still pulling wires on the engine of the snowplow and then shining the light on what he'd done.

"I think it's one of them."

"Just a couple more seconds here." Jason's voice held no hint of the panic she felt. "Hold the light for me."

She shone the light toward his hands. While she appreciated Jason's cool head, she was having a hard time taking in a deep breath. She turned slightly but saw nothing. It would be just a matter of minutes before the thief found them even if he circled the clubhouse first.

Jason clicked something into place, and the engine sputtered to life. Now for sure the noise would send their pursuers toward them. He swung his leg over and got on. Isabel slipped in behind him before he had even settled in the seat. After he lifted the plow, the ATV lurched forward.

A gunshot echoed behind them. Isabel leaned close to Jason and held on tight. Jason steered around the building toward the road. But instead of taking the road, he cut across it down the hill. Smart. The car would only be able to traverse the road.

Another gunshot resounded behind them. Isabel held on to Jason even tighter. Her heart pounded wildly as adrenaline surged through her.

Behind her, the car engine started up. As Jason maneuvered the ATV straight downhill, the roar of the car seemed to press in on them from all sides. The snow grew deeper, slowing their progress. They might get stuck. They had no choice. Jason veered the snowmobile back onto the road.

The headlights from the car encapsulated them. Jason switched up a gear and increased his speed. They were risking an accident, but the ATV was able to progress on the unplowed road faster than the car. They slipped out of the grasp of the headlights as Jason put a little distance between them and their pursuer.

He cut off the road and headed straight downhill again. The ATV caught air and landed hard. Pain shot up Isabel's back but she held on. She peered over Jason's shoulder. Up ahead was a cluster of trees. Jason slowed as they drew close. He wove through the trees. As he lost speed, the noise of the ATV motor kicked down a notch. The hum of the car engine in the still night reached her ears. She could see the flash of headlights through the trees.

Fear squeezed her stomach into a tight knot. The car couldn't follow them into the trees, but they were going so slow, he could cut them off when they came back out on the road.

Jason steered sideways and continued to navigate through the labyrinth of the trees. The sound of the car faded into the distance. Gradually, the landscape became more open and flat. The ATV picked up speed once again.

When she looked to one side, the faint outline of the Wilsons' house was visible up the hill. They'd gone in a circle. Jason drove the ATV toward the road she'd come up hours earlier in her car. She took in a deep breath. It was only a couple of miles down the hill until the private road intersected with the two-lane that would take them back into town.

Jason didn't slow down when he got to the road. She caught the glimpse of headlights in her peripheral vision. They weren't home free yet. The car was still following them.

The exposed skin on Jason's face tingled from the wind and snow hitting it as he couched low. Though he couldn't hear the car, he knew it had made it to the road they were on and was still chasing them.

He revved the throttle. Isabel pressed close to him as he gained speed. He could feel the pressure of her arms around his waist though they both wore too many layers of clothing to feel her body heat. He liked having her so close. Maybe now she'd come to trust him.

With the motor humming, they descended the hill. The ATV seemed to almost hover over the snow, providing them with a smooth ride.

Isabel leaned close to his ear and shouted, "He's getting closer."

They must be within a half mile of the two-lane road. He turned the handlebars and directed the ATV toward the bumpier, more foreboding landscape where a car would not be able to follow.

He aimed toward a patch of trees, swerving expertly around them. The rough terrain didn't scare him. He'd grown up riding ATVs and dirt bikes with his father. The ATV headlights cut a swath of light in front of him so he could plan his next move.

Chances were the thief would patrol the two-lane and wait for them to emerge, but he could only go back and forth on a small section of road at a time. If he took the ATV far enough out they'd be able to get on the two-lane without being spotted.

A steep drop on the hillside caused them to catch air again. As they sailed through the air, he tried to maneuver the machine for a successful landing. The nose of the ATV pointed downward. Isabel screamed but held on tight.

They dived into a snowbank. The crash seemed to make all his bones vibrate.

He took in a breath and patted Isabel's gloved hand. "Are you okay?"

"I don't think anything is broken."

The motor of the snowmobile had died. "Can you get off? I've got to see if I can get this thing started and out of this snowbank." He was still a little shaky from the impact of the crash.

Isabel swung her leg over and stepped back. She pulled his keys out and shone the light for Jason.

"It looks pretty stuck." Her voice was monotone, devoid of any emotion.

Maybe she was just as exhausted as he was from all the running.

Fragments of light flashed below them, a car going by on the two-lane.

He lifted his head and met Isabel's gaze. Was she thinking the same thing he was? "This time of night there won't be many cars going by." Even fewer because of the storm.

"I still think it's our best shot." Her voice filled with resolve. "Maybe the snowplows are out by now. We can flag one down."

It was a huge risk. They'd have to dodge the thief in the big car and hope that another vehicle came along. "We can't stay here." The ATV was dead. Either the cold or the thief would be their demise.

Isabel held the flashlight in such a way that it illuminated her face. She nodded, but he saw the fear in her eyes.

"We'll stay in the trees as much as possible."

He reached a gloved hand out for hers. She lifted her hand and he squeezed it, hoping the gesture would help quell her fear.

He turned. "Only use the flashlight when you absolutely need to. It makes us too easy to spot. The bright colors of my coat will draw attention too."

"I can turn it inside out." She slipped out of his coat and turned it to the dark lining.

He started walking. She trudged behind him. He breathed in a silent prayer that a car would come by sooner rather than later. Though the storm was no longer raging, staying out in the cold for any length of time would not be a good idea.

He was unable to see the ground clearly, so his footsteps were slow and measured. Isabel whispered something.

He kept walking but turned his head slightly. "What did you say?"

"Oh sorry. I didn't realize you could hear me. I was…praying."

"Yeah, we could use some of that." He felt closer to her, knowing that she'd thought to pray.

"Sometimes things have to be at their darkest before I think of it," she said.

He opened his mouth to answer but stopped when he spotted headlights through the trees. The car eased along the road. Most likely it was the thief searching for them. He crouched and Isabel slipped in beside him. The car stopped and the driver got out. Shining his flashlight, the man peered up into the trees where he and Isabel were hiding. It was clearly the thief. He must have seen their flashlight when they had it on. The thief continued to walk toward them in a zigzag pattern.

The car engine still hummed. The thief had left it running to keep the engine warm.

An idea sparked inside Jason's head. They could get to the thief's car and drive it to safety.

Jason squeezed Isabel's arm just above the elbow and tilted his head. She nodded in under-standing. They'd be spotted if they went straight for the car. Still crouching, he moved from tree to tree, working his way down to the road in an arc. Isabel stayed close.

The thief's light bobbed through the forest maybe twenty yards from where they were. Jason scanned the landscape below. It was hard to discern much of anything. He chose his path and made a run for it, knowing that Isabel would be right behind him. He put his foot forward but found only air.

The hill dropped off abruptly. He lost his balance. He tumbled, rolling through the snow. He righted himself. The chill of the snow soaked through his skin. Isabel came to a stop beside him.

A gunshot reverberated through the silence as the light came toward them. The noise of the fall had been enough for the thief to find them. Cold and wet, he grabbed Isabel's hand and made a run for it, coming out on the road behind the running car.

Another gunshot stirred up snow in front of them. Isabel stumbled. He pulled her toward the car. The thief emerged from the trees, lifting his gun. Jason pulled Isabel to the ground as the third shot whizzed over them.

She bolted to her feet and raced toward the car. Jason pulled his gun from his waistband and fired a shot to deter the thief. He didn't want anybody to die here tonight.

The thief dodged back toward a tree. Isabel climbed into the driver's seat and slammed the door. Jason raced toward the car, grabbing the back-door handle as Isabel eased the car forward. He jumped in as another gunshot shattered the back window. Jason stayed low in the seat. Isabel hit the gas and sped down the road.

They'd have to turn around and go past the thief one more time if they were to get to town. The car rumbled down the road. Though it swerved on the unplowed pavement, Isabel kept it moving.

Jason glanced at the shattered back window.

Isabel stared straight ahead. "Just looking for a place to get turned around." Her calmness surprised him. She waited until she found a shoulder and performed a three-point turn with ease.

"Nice driving."

"Thanks. I've had a little experience."

He wondered what she meant by that. "He'll be waiting for us."

She focused on the road in front of her. "I know, but there is no other way off this mountain."

He liked that she was so cool under pressure. They rounded a curve. They weren't far from where they'd left the shooter. Jason pulled his gun out, rolled the window down and then crouched low in the back seat. Isabel did the same, though she had to stay high enough to see the road.

He listened to the rhythm of the car's tires rolling over the compressed snow where they'd driven before while he watched the trees for a flash of light or movement. He held his breath.

Isabel increased the speed of the car.

Tension threaded through his chest as he rested the barrel of the gun on the windowsill.

A single gunshot boomed through the air. Jason caught a flare of gunfire by the trees close to the road. He aimed his gun in that direction. The car fishtailed and swerved.

"I think he must have hit the radiator or something vital." Isabel sounded like she was speaking through gritted teeth. "I'm going to take this thing as far as it will go."

The car limped along down the dark road. The engine began to chug and then quit altogether.

Isabel sat behind the wheel, staring out at the darkness.

After a long moment, Jason said, "There must be a house between here and town."

"Not on the main road there isn't," she said.

"Maybe hidden back in the trees. We'd see the lights at this hour."

"Maybe." Isabel nodded. "There's that convenience store that sells fishing supplies in the summer. Maybe the owner lives there. Must be a couple of miles. Course, everything seems closer when you're driving."

A heaviness seemed to descend into the car. All of these ideas for getting to safety were long shots at best.

He pushed open his door, stepped out and reached for Isabel's door handle. Preparing to trek through the snow—again—he didn't need to see her face clearly to know that she was feeling the same despair as he was.

They hurried down the road, both of them looking over their shoulders from time to time. Maybe they had gotten enough of a head start on the thief to outrun him. Jason's feet padded on the fluffy snow. He scanned the area around them, peering through the trees for any sign of a dwelling. Isabel trudged beside him, her shoulders slumping forward.

"We're going to make it." Jason tried to sound upbeat. "We've made it this far."

She just kept lumbering ahead.

At one point, he had a view of the road below them with the switchbacks. No sign of any cars. The storm had dumped a ton of snow. Though no rational civilian would go out at this hour after such a downfall, he'd hoped to maybe see snowplows or the highway patrol.

Snow swirled out of the dark sky. Under different circumstances, the scene would have seemed almost serene.

Isabel stopped and turned toward the forest. "I thought I saw a light."

He followed the line of her gaze as a lump formed in his throat. Seconds ticked by and he saw only the shadowy outline of the trees. Was this just wishful thinking on her part?

"There." She grabbed his arm just above the elbow and pointed with her free hand.

He still didn't see anything. "Isabel, I—"

"I know what I saw." She planted her feet and continued to stare.

He glanced up the road, half expecting to see their pursuer. He caught the flash of illumination and turned to where Isabel was looking.

A light emerged from the trees and seemed to be gliding across the landscape. A cross-country skier with a headlamp and reflective clothing.

Isabel took off running. She shouted. The skier stopped, turned and came toward them.

Isabel spoke breathlessly. "Can you help us? Our car went off the road."

With her hat and gear on, it was hard to judge the skier's age. She wore a reflective vest that looked official. Her gaze moved from Isabel to Jason.

"Are you avalanche patrol?" Jason asked, hoping to allay the woman's suspicions.

"Yes. With all the snowfall, I thought I'd better get out and have a look. Plus, there's nothing in the world like skiing at night in the silence."

"Please, if we could just use your phone."

The desperation in Isabel's voice must have won the woman over. "My place is back through the trees. You can call, but I wouldn't recommend anyone come get you until the plows have been up this way. They get them out as soon as the storm lets up, so I would say another hour or so."

The woman led them back to a small trailer that had been skirted around the bottom to keep the plumbing from freezing. They followed her into the tiny space. The woman tore her hat off, revealing braids and a bright smile. She probably wasn't more than twenty.

She did a half turn in her trailer. "It's not much. But they pay me to ski, so I can't complain." She grabbed a phone off the counter and handed it to Jason. "You'll have to go outside to get a signal. I'll put a kettle on for tea."

Jason took the phone and stepped outside.

His contact at the Bureau would be the best choice. That way he could run the idea of going undercover past them. They'd been through a lot tonight, but maybe he could turn it around for the best.

The biggest concern was Isabel. She didn't need to be caught up in the middle of this, but the thieves had seen her. Even now he felt himself drawn to her. She was a hard person to read. That kind of complexity intrigued him. More than anything, he wanted to protect her.

His contact picked up on the third ring. "Michael?"

"Hey, Jason, we were starting to worry about you."

Jason gave the edited version of what had happened and his approximate location. Michael agreed to send an agent to pick them up and decided on a location to meet them when they got to town. He and Isabel would probably have to hike out to the road to be seen. He'd have to make arrangements for his van to be towed from the location.

When he clicked off the phone, he was surprised to see Isabel standing in front of him. Her arms crossed over her chest.

"My friend will come and get us."

"You owe me an explanation for what happened here tonight. I could lose my job for the mess that house was left in."

Yes, things might work out for the best with the investigation. But then there was the problem of Isabel's safety and her demand to know more.

SEVEN

It was still dark when Jason's friend picked them up. The echo of the snowplows clearing the roads seemed to be everywhere. From the vantage point on the mountain where they stood waiting, Isabel could see three sets of headlights clearing different roads of the snow.

A truck approached them and slowed.

Jason waved and the truck came to a stop. He opened the door for her to get into the front seat and then climbed in beside her.

"Thanks for coming to get us, Larry," Jason said.

"No problem." Larry had graying temples and a beak-like nose. Though he wore a ski jacket, something about him seemed very formal or official in some way.

Back at the trailer, Jason had still not offered her an explanation that made sense. He'd been evasive.

She didn't think he was a criminal or up to

no good anymore. He'd kept her alive at the risk of his own safety and stayed with her through everything. Why, then, was he keeping secrets from her?

They were squeezed like sardines in the cab of the truck.

She let out a heavy breath, relaxing for the first time since she'd had a knife put to her throat at the Wilsons' house.

"I can't wait to go home, take a hot shower and get some sleep." A few hours, anyway. She had some explaining to do to her boss about the condition the Wilsons' home had been left in. The broken vase in the entryway, the shattered window in the studio... The groceries she was supposed to stock were still in her car, which was wedged against a tree. Her stomach clenched. Would she even have a job after all this? She couldn't tell Mary the truth. It sounded too outrageous. Always there was the fear that because she had a record, she would be suspected if any crime took place in her proximity. Mary had been nothing but supportive of her, but other people hadn't been so kind.

"Actually, Isabel, I need you to come with me." Jason's gaze darted to Larry. "Can you drop us off at Ralph's Café? I'll borrow your phone and have Michael meet us there."

Larry nodded and handed over his phone.

Really, their interactions didn't seem like they were friends, more like coworkers. And who was this Michael person and what was Jason up to? Her stomach tightened. "Wait a minute. I need to get home. I have to be at work in four hours. And I don't have access to a car anymore."

Jason gripped her hand. "This is important for both our sakes."

Something in the force of his voice told her protest would be futile.

She pressed her back against the seat. "Just for the record, I need to keep this job and I need a car that runs."

They drove toward town in silence as a dozen anxious thoughts whirled through Isabel's head. She'd been so focused on staying alive, she hadn't had time to process what all that had happened meant for her future. By this afternoon, the Wilsons would be arriving to a home that was in disarray—or worse, where the thieves were hiding out. She needed to make sure the Wilsons weren't going into an unsafe situation.

"I'll go with you, but you have to let me call my boss in a little bit." Mary wouldn't be waking up for at least another hour, well before the Wilsons were set to arrive.

"We can do that." Jason nodded and then

pressed the numbers on the phone and spoke to the man he called Michael.

Anxious thoughts pounded through her mind. What would she tell Mary? That thieves had been in the house, and she'd had to flee. The short version would be the best. Still nervous, she laced her gloved hands together.

They pulled up to an all-night café on the edge of town. Jason opened the passenger-side door, thanked Larry and held out a hand for Isabel to step down from the big truck.

He locked onto her with his blue eyes, watching her. "I'm sorry about all of this," he said.

The soft features of his face, the warmth of his voice. He seemed so sincere.

"Please, my job is very important to me."

He took her hand and led her toward the café. "I'm going to try to get this straightened out."

They went inside the café. Only a waitress and the cook were inside. Jason chose a corner booth.

"Are you hungry?"

"Starving." Her stomach rumbled on cue.

The waitress, who had orange hair, sauntered toward them. She had to be at least in her seventies. "What can I get you two?"

They both ordered burgers and milkshakes.

A car pulled into the parking lot. A moment later, a tall man got out and stepped inside. He held a computer. Jason rose to his feet. "I need to talk to Michael alone."

More secrets.

A weariness settled into Isabel's muscles. She needed sleep. The two men took a booth at the other end of the room with Michael facing her. The older man flipped open his computer and started typing while Jason spoke to him. Jason pulled out the bookmark wrapped in cardboard and handed it over to Michael. The conversation went on for several minutes with Jason doing most of the talking. Though she couldn't hear what they were saying, she could read lips enough to know that Michael had said, "Sun and Ski Property Management." He glanced in Isabel's direction and then proceeded to type on his keypad.

Jason turned his head to look at her. Though she believed Jason could be trusted, suspicion and fear niggled at the corners of her mind. She'd trusted Nick Solomon too. She hadn't dated since Nick, fearing that she might only be able to attract another bad boy. Jason and Michael caused that doubt to come back into her head. Not that she saw him as dating material, but what if she was wrong about Jason? Why was he insisting that she stay close and not letting her go home? What if he was up to no good?

* * *

While Michael pulled up files pertinent to the investigation, Jason tried to push past the tension knotting the muscles in his neck. Would the Bureau be open to the idea of his going undercover or would he be out of a job after tonight's fiasco?

After a moment, Michael spoke while still staring at the computer screen. "I thought the name Sun and Ski Property Management sounded familiar. It seems they manage a lot of the properties where the thefts have taken place." He glanced toward Isabel. "Are you sure your new friend can be trusted?"

He'd spent a harrowing night with her, both of them fighting for each other's lives. "I believe so, yes."

"Maybe she's clean, but that doesn't mean Sun and Ski isn't somehow involved." Michael scratched his chin. "They would certainly know when houses were vacant and have security codes."

"If we could just get her some protection. She saw the thieves more clearly than I did, and they can probably identify her."

"You said that the thieves think the two of you are partners."

"Yes, but it's too dangerous to ask her to become involved in the investigation," Jason said.

"Look, find out what her last name is. We'll run a check on her. Meanwhile hang close to her and see what you can find out about Sun and Ski. That will give her some protection. The couriers are pretty low-level thugs. Chances are their desire for revenge will blow over in twenty-four hours."

"I'm not so sure. They were pretty determined. And now they think we've horned in on their profit margin and can identify them," said Jason.

"Take her to the city police station and see if she can identify the two men she saw at the house. Maybe we can get them picked up for something else."

"Isabel deserves an explanation. All she knows is that I'm a PI."

"For now, we need to keep her in the dark," Michael said.

The waitress moved across the floor, holding two plates, but hesitated when she saw Jason at a different table.

"Why don't you go eat?" Michael closed his computer. "I'll make arrangements for a ride." He tossed a set of keys on the table. "You take her down to the police station."

Jason motioned for the waitress to take the plates over to where Isabel waited. He grabbed the keys and returned to where Isabel was already slathering ketchup on her burger.

He sat opposite her. The aroma of the burger made his mouth water and his stomach rumble.

"Is that guy a policeman?" She took a bite, closing her eyes while she chewed, savoring the taste.

There was something endearing about the way she enjoyed her food.

Jason shifted in his chair. "I still can't explain everything to you."

"Secrets make me nervous."

"It's for your protection. Please take my word for that."

She picked up a fry and popped it into her mouth while her gaze rested on him. She didn't speak until she finished chewing the fry. "Your word has been good so far."

He relaxed a little. At least she'd chosen to trust him. "We need to go down to the police station to identify the two guys you saw at the house. You got a better look at them than I did." He didn't want to worry her that she might still be a target.

"Fine, but I need to swing by work and talk to my boss first. She gets into the office bright and early. Plus, I've got to find a way to get my car back into town."

"Okay, we can do that." Driving her around

gave him the excuse he needed to stay close until he was sure the thieves wouldn't come after her.

They finished their meal and got into the car Michael had loaned him. The sun was low on the horizon as they drove through Silver Strike, which featured lots of boutique-type shops. Isabel gave Jason directions that led them to the Sun and Ski headquarters, a Victorian house that had been converted to offices. The sign said that a real-estate company also had an office in the building.

As they pulled into the lot, she turned to face him. "I live upstairs. Mary, my boss, was nice enough to rent the one bedroom to me at a low rate." Despite her blond hair being a little disheveled, Isabel still had the demeanor of someone who had come from money. He wondered what her story was. Why she was so hard to get a clear read on.

"You like your job and your boss." Sun and Ski was under suspicion. That meant this Mary person wasn't off the hook yet.

"Yes." Her smile lit up her whole face.

"That's the first time I've seen you smile."

"It's the first time I've had a reason to smile since you met me." She let out a laugh that reminded him of songbirds.

"Indeed." For having known each other for

such a short time, they'd been through a lot. The moment of connection between them seemed to make the car warmer and brighter. Guilt washed through him. He wished he could come clean with her. "Let's go inside."

She pushed open the door, taking in an intense breath. "I've got a lot of explaining to do to Mary for the condition of the house. The Wilsons will be there soon."

He followed her into an office that had three desks. A fortyish woman with coppery hair stood by one of the workstations, her purse slung over her shoulder.

"Isabel, I'm about to run out to a house but I'm glad I caught up with you." Her gaze rested on Jason.

Isabel glanced at Jason. "This is my friend. He gave me a ride."

Mary furrowed her eyebrows. "Yes, I was just on the phone to the Wilsons. They got into town earlier than expected. I guess they told you they wouldn't be here until the afternoon."

"But they are safe?" said Isabel.

"Safe?" Mary looked perplexed. "Why wouldn't they be? They said the house was in order. Only they wondered why your car was parked down the road and how the vase got broken. They found the shards in the garbage."

"The house was in order?" The Wilsons must

not have seen the studio's broken window or found her clothes in Victoria's closet.

"You are a great employee and I am sure there is an explanation for all this. I'd love to hear it when I have more time." Mary tilted her head. "The problem I'm having, Isabel, is that they texted your personal phone to say they were coming early. All client calls need to go through Sun and Ski, regardless of what your relationship is with them. I need to know if one of our clients has had a change of plans."

"I understand. I'm sorry." Isabel hung her head. "I guess I was too focused on trying to keep the clients happy."

Someone must have picked the thieves up. Maybe they'd taken the time to remove all traces that they'd been in the house to protect the smuggling operation.

"I need to run. I'll catch up with you in a bit." Mary winked at Isabel and patted her shoulder. "I do appreciate your going up there on your day off." Mary hurried out the door. Her anger over Isabel not keeping her in the loop about the Wilsons' early arrival set off alarm bells for Jason.

Isabel shook her head. "I don't know what's going on here. Why the place was cleaned up. Mary didn't say anything about your van being there."

He suspected the Bureau had already been

up there to have it towed. "It's just good that everything worked out."

"No, it's weird that everything worked out." She studied him for a long moment, as if expecting him to explain further. The phone rang. She picked up. "Sun and Ski Property Management. This is Isabel speaking. How may I help you?"

Isabel listened for a moment. Her face drained of color and she slammed the phone down.

He took a step toward her. "What is it?"

Fear permeated each word she uttered. "That was…a man. He said I have something he wants. And that I better give it back or pay with my life."

EIGHT

Jason had a hard time focusing on the road as they drove across town to the police station. Any hope he had about Isabel being safe had been removed. Maybe now she wouldn't be upset if he chose to keep close to her until he could get her some protection.

Had it been the thieves who phoned or someone higher up in the smuggling ring?

He glanced over at Isabel. She offered him a nervous smile and then stared out the window. The problem was someone in the ring had contacted Isabel first. Either because they hadn't figured out who he was or because she was the more vulnerable one. How was he going to get her out of this mess and make sure she wouldn't be harmed? Maybe the threat would be enough for Michael to be motivated to spring for some protection.

"How do you suppose they figured out who I was?"

"Is there anything in your car that would have helped them trace you back to Sun and Ski?"

"There's a logo on the back window. And my picture and name is on our website." Her voice filled with fear.

He hadn't noticed the logo.

He braked at a stoplight and studied her for a moment. Her fingers were laced together in her lap so tight that her knuckles had turned white.

"I'm sorry that you got dragged into all this."

"I can't live my life looking over my shoulder. A lot of the properties we manage are out in the middle of nowhere."

"Look, I don't have a lot going on. I'll stay with you through your workday if you don't mind my tagging along." He kind of liked the idea of being with her.

The light turned green. He rolled through the street checking his rearview mirror. A dark car that had been behind them before followed them as he clicked his blinker and turned up a side street. He didn't want to alarm Isabel. She was already scared enough.

She unlaced her fingers and rested her hands palm down in her lap. "You would do that for me?"

"Sure."

"Guess I was just in the wrong place at the wrong time. I thought what I was doing was giving a hundred and ten percent to my job. That totally backfired."

This was his chance to do a little probing. "Yes, your boss seemed more than a little miffed you didn't keep her in the loop."

"She's not usually like that. She's been very good to me."

"I just wonder why she was so upset, then."

She stared at him long enough to make him nervous. "I was in the wrong. I went against our standard practice. She's a good person."

Jason checked the rearview mirror. The car was still behind them.

"I see him too," Isabel said, her voice barely above a whisper.

He turned on the street that led to the police station. The car veered onto a side street. Once it was clear, Jason pulled into the police-station parking lot. No one was going to bother them when they were surrounded by a half dozen armed officers…he hoped, anyway.

Isabel appreciated the supportive hand Jason placed on her back as they entered the police station. She felt like she'd been trembling from terror ever since the phone call at Sun and Ski. Having him close at least helped her take a deep breath.

"Hey, Jason." One of the police officers

waved at them as they entered the station. He stepped toward them. "What brings you here?"

"This is Isabel…?" He turned toward her raising an eyebrow.

"Connor. My last name is Connor."

"She needs to do an ID for me. You got your file of petty criminals loaded up?"

"Sure. Come this way." The officer held out a hand to her. "I'm Officer Nelson. Jason and I went to high school together about fifty miles down the road in a little town no one has heard of."

Isabel shook Officer Nelson's hand.

"Come right this way." Officer Nelson gestured.

She glanced over at Jason. "You're not coming with me?"

"I've got a call to make." He didn't quite make eye contact. "You'll be fine."

Officer Nelson led her to a desk where he opened up a laptop computer. "So you were a witness to a crime and Jason is helping you?" He clicked several keys until a police photo of a man came up on the screen.

"Something like that."

He bent to reach the keyboard. "Just click here to see the next photo." Officer Nelson squeezed her shoulder. "Holler if you have any trouble."

She filed through half a dozen photographs,

studying each one. A picture of her old boy-friend Nick Solomon flashed on the screen. Her cheeks flushed as shame rose to the surface. She glanced around the police station, feeling as if everyone else would know she had once been connected with this petty thief.

Even in the police photo, Nick offered the camera his crooked smile and big brown eyes. She'd been so naive back then.

Her eyes came to rest on Jason, who was talking on an office phone. When he saw her staring, he turned away. The old quiver of suspicion and distrust returned. She wanted to believe he was a good guy. Everything he'd done and said so far backed that up. His kindness in offering to stay with her warmed her heart. But the look he gave her seemed filled with suspicion.

She stared at the photo of Nick again. What she didn't trust was her own judgment of character with men. She had such a lousy track record.

Officer Nelson walked by her, holding a stack of file folders. "Is everything going okay?"

"So far I haven't seen either of the men." She was still on edge from the phone call. Seeing Nick in all his criminal glory hadn't helped. "Actually, I need a minute to freshen up and clear my head. Where's your bathroom?"

"You'll have to use the one downstairs at the

end of the hall. The one on this floor is part of a construction zone."

Isabel pushed her chair back. She stared through the window at Jason, who was still on the phone. He looked at her. Something in his expression had changed. He looked...pensive?

She hurried down the hallway past scaffolding, toolboxes and cans of paint. But no workers. They must be on a break. The downstairs was quiet. The signs on the doors indicated the rooms were used mostly for storage of records and evidence.

She slipped into the bathroom and splashed water on her face, then stared at herself in the mirror. She looked frazzled, had dark circles under her eyes.

Come on, Izzy. Pull it together.

She bent her head and squeezed her eyes shut. "If God is for me, who can be against me?"

The door to the bathroom swung open. Before she had time to see who it was, a hand grabbed her hair and a knife was at her throat.

"You have something I want."

She shook her head, then tried to turn toward the mirror to see the man who held her captive. He pressed the knife deeper into her skin.

"Don't lie to me. You have twenty-four hours. We'll give you a drop-off point." He shoved her toward the wall and she fell. By the time she righted herself, she was alone in the bathroom.

She stood frozen and listening. Was the man with the knife waiting just outside the door? Her heart pounded wildly in her chest. She could manage only shallow breaths.

Isabel stepped toward the door and pushed it open. She peered up and down the empty hallway before stepping out.

Pounding footsteps made her turn to retreat back into the bathroom until she saw Jason at the bottom of the stairs.

She ran toward him. His expression registered that he saw how scared she was. He held out his arms to her.

"Hey, what happened?"

"They found me." Her voice was hoarse. Her words came out in broken fragments.

She rested against the soft flannel of Jason's shirt. His arms surrounded her, and she was able to take in a deep breath.

After a long moment of silence, he said. "I had a feeling when you didn't come right back. I hate that this is happening to you."

She pulled back and gazed into his blue eyes. "They want the bookmark. I have twenty-four hours. They are supposed to contact me with a location." Her chest felt like it was in a corset being pulled tighter and tighter.

"Could you tell if it was one of the men from the house?"

She shook her head. "I didn't see him. I don't have a good memory for voices and he didn't say much."

He took her hand and led her to a bench in the hallway. She sat down beside him. It still felt like someone was rattling her spine.

"I wish that they had gotten in touch with me. But it's you they want to deal with."

"What are you talking about?"

"I was on the phone to Michael." He studied her for a moment. His mouth twitched. There was something he was keeping from her.

"Who is he, anyway—your boss?"

"He's an FBI agent. Since you got the threat on the phone, he gave me permission to share with you what is going on. I'm helping the FBI investigate a smuggling ring that often uses empty homes as a drop-off point. We're building profiles of all the people involved to try to get to whoever is behind it all."

She rose to her feet. "I don't want to be involved with any of this. I just want to go back to my job, back to my life."

He stood up and grabbed her hands. "I understand." He squeezed her fingers. "But I need to hang with you until they contact you…for your safety."

She knew he was right about that. She couldn't just go about her day as if nothing had happened. She needed his protection. "I don't like associating with criminals in any way, shape or form. Michael has the bookmark. The two of you can work this out."

"I will do everything I can to keep you out of harm's way and try to work it so they will deal with me."

His expression looked so sincere. "What are you going to do? Follow me around like a puppy?"

"Actually, I prefer the term *guard dog*." The corners of his mouth turned up.

His joke made her smile. "I guess this is the way it has to be. I need to head home to take a shower and get some sleep and then I have to go to work."

"I'll go with you to the houses when you set them up. You don't have a car anyway."

She pressed her hands against her mouth and stared at the ceiling. "I don't like any of this. I don't like being around…criminals."

"I think I understand." He locked eyes with her. "I know about your record. Even though it was sealed, the FBI has ways of finding these things out."

So that was why he'd looked at her that way. Her cheeks grew warm. "That was a long time ago. I was seventeen." She turned away from him as a sense of deep shame rose to the surface. "I'm not one of them anymore. And I don't want anything to do with thieves."

He touched the back of her arm. "I know you're not. I can see that you've made changes. Only someone who's turned her life over to God would have been praying while being chased. Michael had concerns, but I vouched for you."

She turned to face him, feeling tears rise up in the corners of her eyes. "You vouched for me?" Warmth pooled around her heart. Sometimes she felt like having been a juvenile delinquent in a small community where everybody knew your history flashed like a neon sign around her. So few people believed in her aside from Mary, her pastor, a few friends and now Jason. "Thank you."

He nodded. "Now let's drive you back to your place so you can get some sleep."

Snow twirled out of the sky as they drove back to Sun and Ski. The plows had worked through the morning creating walls of snow on either side of the city streets. They stopped at a store so she and Jason could buy new phones.

Jason parked the car outside the Sun and Ski office.

"You can come in and get some rest on the

couch. You're probably tired too." The truth was she felt better knowing that he was close.

Isabel led him up the stairs to her place. She put her key in the lock and pushed open the door. The house was old and not well insulated. The top floor could get chilly but she'd done her best to make it cozy with lace curtains as well as a quilt thrown over the worn red velvet couch.

"Nice, very homey," said Jason turning a half circle.

It made her feel good that he liked her little apartment. His opinion was starting to matter to her.

"Make yourself at home. There's sandwich stuff and tea and coffee. I feel like I could sleep for a hundred years."

She took a quick shower and crawled in under her comforter. Heavy curtains blocked out the light. She closed her eyes, waiting for sleep to come. Her body was beyond tired, but restless, fearful thoughts made it hard for her to shut down her brain.

She'd worked so hard to cut ties with her past. Though Jason believed in her, any thought of associating with criminals brought up all the pain from her teenage years. She drew her comforter up to her neck. These men could be violent. Would they leave her alone once she delivered the bookmark or would she always be looking over her shoulder?

The only thing that eased her troubled mind was knowing that Jason was in the next room. She was safe...for now.

NINE

Jason collapsed on Isabel's couch. He pulled out his phone and dialed Michael's number to tell him about Isabel being attacked at the police station. The thieves were probably going after Isabel because she was the easier target...more vulnerable. That infuriated him.

He summarized for Michael what had happened and then said, "If there is any way we can get her clear of all this, we need to do it. She didn't sign up for this. I did."

Michael's response was measured. "Involving a civilian is never the best approach, but she's knee-deep in this already. I know you're willing to see her motives as pure. I have a wait-and-see policy. The Bureau has found that sometimes criminals can be a help in an investigation. Our end goal is finding out who's behind this operation."

Jason clenched his jaw. "She's not a criminal."

"In the meantime, we're going to put a tail on

her boss and look into Mary Helms's connections. For now, you are Isabel Connor's protection. If you're seen together, it will further the cover that the two of you are thieves working together and maybe you can figure out Sun and Ski's level of involvement, if any."

"I'll let you know when they contact her about the bookmark." Feeling a little frustrated, Jason clicked off the phone. Michael could be really myopic when it came to the investigation. At least this way, Isabel would be safe. He'd see to that. He slumped down on the couch, closed his eyes and pulled his feet onto the couch, allowing the heaviness of sleep to overtake him.

He awoke to the smell of coffee and bacon sizzling in a pan. Isabel was dressed in a long skirt, boots and a sweater. Her honey-blond hair was pulled up into a loose bun. Soft tangles surrounded her face. She looked beautiful.

She offered him a smile. "Feel better?"

He rose to his feet. "Yes. I needed that."

"Coffee is on and I should have a late breakfast ready in just a minute."

He poured himself a cup and wandered around her small living room. Her walls were decorated with cross-stitched Bible verses and nature photos. He picked up one of the photos on the mantel. A boy of about ten smiled at him.

She plated the food. "That's my little brother, Zac."

Isabel must be about twenty-five. "Your mom had kids really far apart."

A shadow seemed to fall across her face. "He's a half brother. But as far as I'm concerned, he's just a precious little brother to me."

There were no other photos that could be family. Only a picture of Isabel with her boss at a picnic, both of them smiling for the camera, and one of Isabel with her arms around two women her age, a cabin in the background surrounded by forest. The women wore matching T-shirts that referenced a church retreat.

She handed him a plate of food. The aroma of bacon made his mouth water. Her brown-eyed gaze rested on him for a moment. "There's no room for a table. I usually eat on the couch."

They sat side by side. Her posture was ramrod straight, her chin slightly lifted. When she'd been afraid and tired, he'd seen a more vulnerable side to Isabel. Now she'd returned to that professional demeanor that had originally made him think she was from money. He thought he was pretty good at seeing past people's facades, but Isabel wore hers like armor. Now he knew why. Maybe she thought the more formal she seemed, the less likely people were to guess she had a record.

He helped her with the dishes and they headed downstairs to the office.

"Mary will have left me a message about which houses I need to get ready." She swung open the door to the office, which was empty.

"Is this door always unlocked?"

"We come and go all day. It's just easier. The real-estate people next door are hardly ever there."

He stared out at the street, wondering if they were being watched.

Tension threaded through Isabel's words. "Guess I should lock it from now on."

"Maybe this will all be over soon." His words held a note of doubt. Would thieves come after her because she could identify them even if they got the bookmark back? He had the feeling the demand for the return of the bookmark was being engineered by someone higher up in the pecking order. It took a level of criminal sophistication and moxie to come after someone in a police station. Maybe even someone with connections to the police or the financial means to bribe their way into what should be a secure building.

The office phone rang.

Jason swung around.

Isabel pressed her lips together. He read fear in her eyes. His heart beat a little faster, and he swallowed to produce some moisture in his mouth. "Go ahead. Answer it."

She remained as still as a statue.

He stepped toward her, his shoulder pressing against hers. "I'll be right here. And I won't leave until I know you're safe."

The stiffness in her body softened. She seemed to draw courage from what he said. She took in a breath and lifted the phone.

Isabel's heart pounded against her rib cage. She steadied her shaking hand. "Hello." It didn't even sound like her voice.

She could hear breathing on the other end of the line.

"Hello," she repeated, her voice growing stronger. She put the phone on speaker so Jason could hear too.

"The Clauson family home. You know it?" The man on the other end of the line had a husky voice.

"Yes." The Clausons were Sun and Ski clients.

"There's a big shindig there. An invite will be waiting for you at the front entrance of the Clauson house. At eight forty-five go to the library.

History of Rome, volume seven, page twenty-five. Got it?"

Her hands were sweating. "Yes."

"Your friend is not invited."

The line went dead.

Isabel threw the phone down as though it was on fire. The memory of everything that had happened at the Wilsons' bombarded her. These people played for keeps. "I can't do this."

From where he stood beside her, Jason brushed his fingers over her arm. "I'll find a way to be at that party. You won't be alone. I need to get a picture of the pickup man anyway. For them to believe that we really are thieves who want in on the action, we'll have to give them the real bookmark."

She shook her head. "He said you weren't invited."

"It's a party with lots of people around," Jason said. "I'll find a way to stay close and not be noticed."

The steadiness of his voice and his expression of unwavering resolve almost convinced her. "I guess if they wanted to hurt me, they would have chosen somewhere remote. Do you suppose they'll leave me alone if I give the bookmark back?"

His forehead wrinkled with concern. "I'm

not sure. I'll stay with you until we know you're not a target."

"I want this to be over."

Before he could reply, the door burst open and Mary stepped inside.

"Glad to see you're ready to work." She turned toward Jason. "And you still have your driver, I see. I called the tow truck to get your car off the mountain." Mary leaned over and rummaged through a desk drawer until she pulled out a key ring with multiple keys on it. "The atmosphere is like a funeral in here. Isabel, is there something you want to tell me?"

"I'm… I'm just glad to be back at work." She gave Jason a nervous glance, wishing she could tell Mary the whole story.

"Good. We've got a couple of houses to get ready. One of them is a new client. I texted you the instructions. I gotta run."

Mary was out the door. Isabel watched through the big bay window as Mary got into her car and drove off. A moment later, a car pulled away from the curb and fell in behind Mary.

Isabel's breath hitched. "Are you having my boss tailed?"

Jason didn't answer right away. "We have to rule her out. A lot of the houses where the drop-offs happened were managed by Sun and Ski. Mary would have the alarm codes."

"You don't know her. She's been good to me." That the FBI suspected Mary bothered Isabel even more than their suspicion of her.

"It wasn't my call. They just need to rule her out."

From the pit of her roiling stomach, Isabel could feel her resolve coming together. "I'll make this drop if it will help further the investigation and get Mary off the hook. She's innocent."

Jason's face brightened. His eyes held a twinkle. "Thank you for being so brave."

She wasn't so sure it was courage she felt so much as a desire to have all this be over. To get back to the life she'd built for herself, to not have a shadow of suspicion cast over a person she cared about very much.

"How are you going to get into the fund-raiser?"

"I have some connections. Big event like that is most likely catered. The Bureau will no doubt plant some people in there too. You're not alone in this, Isabel."

The words were like a soothing balm to her.

Jason gave her shoulder a supportive squeeze. "Well, come on. I'll take you to the houses you need to open up and then you have a ball gown to buy, Cinderella."

TEN

Jason felt itchy and uncomfortable in the waiter's uniform his friend had loaned him. Starched white shirt, tails and cummerbund were not his style. He was a jeans and flannel or wool shirt kind of guy. He tugged on his collar as he scanned the room and kept his eye on the door, looking for Isabel.

"Thank you." A tall woman in a sparkling gown grabbed a glass off his tray. Her dress was the same color as the champagne he served.

He spotted one other Bureau guy as he wove through the room. One of the older agents, a short man with a widow's peak, stood talking to a man in a cowboy hat.

Isabel had ten more minutes before she had to make the drop. She ought to have shown up by now. His heart squeezed a little tighter.

Jason had stayed with Isabel through the day and into evening.

After they'd found her a dress and picked up

the bookmark from Michael, he'd dropped her off at her place to get ready with the understanding that she would text him when she left. He'd had to get to the party to be in place when she arrived. Her text had come through ten minutes ago. How long did it take to get across town? Had it been a mistake to leave her even for that short time? What if the fund-raiser party was just a ruse and they intended to grab her the first chance they got?

He checked his watch one more time. He needed to get into place in the library without being noticed. He had to assume the smuggler mastermind had planted people besides the pickup guy among the partygoers. Even if the smuggler had figured out who Jason was, the waiter's uniform would make him invisible.

Isabel appeared suddenly at the door, dressed in royal blue.

Jason breathed a sigh of relief.

Her cheeks were flushed with color. Her skin had something on it that sparkled when she stepped into the light and down the stairs. She looked stunning.

She spotted him but made only momentary eye contact. She wove through the crowd, stopping to shake hands and talk to people. A lot of these people were probably clients.

She whisked past him.

He spoke under his breath. "Everything go okay?"

"Yes, but I think I was followed. I had to take the long way."

Might have been the thieves they'd encountered at the Wilsons'. The higher-ups would have known she was headed to the fund-raiser.

The music stopped, and a woman picked up a microphone to make announcements about the money raised and silent-auction items still left to be bid on. While the attention of the crowd was on the woman, Jason set his tray down and headed toward the library. Isabel had explained the layout of the house to him earlier in the evening.

Knowing that a nervous glance might give him away, he kept his gaze on the stairs in front of him but listened to make sure he wasn't followed. The library was on the second story at the opposite end of the house, far away from any partygoers. Even someone who was lost or looking for a bathroom wouldn't be on that side of the house.

In order to make the drop, Isabel would be less than a minute or two behind him. They were cutting this pretty close. His heart kicked into high gear and adrenaline surged through his system.

The library was dark. He slipped behind a desk and waited for the sound of Isabel's footsteps. In this light, it would be nearly impossible to identify the pickup man. Jason would have to follow him back into the throng of partygoers and look for an opportunity to snap a photo. If that opportunity didn't arise, he'd have to get a good look at the guy and trust his memory.

All Isabel had to do was slip the bookmark into place and hurry back to the crowd. She'd be safe among the partygoers.

He heard the light tapping of footsteps on the wood floor outside. Isabel's dress made swishing sounds as she entered the room. She did a half turn in the middle of the floor, probably wondering where he was hiding.

His heart lurched. He wanted to say something to let her know he had her back. But it was too risky. She approached the bookshelf and clicked the light on her phone, bending close to the volumes. She held a gold clutch purse that contained the bookmark.

A shadow entered the room from a side door. The man was so silent and quick, Jason heard only two footsteps before the dark figure grabbed Isabel and spun her around, whispering something sinister-sounding in her ear.

Jason jumped to his feet and hurried toward

Isabel. The shadow swung around so Isabel was between him and Jason.

"I've got a gun on her. You come any closer, she takes a bullet."

He couldn't see a gun, and though he was less than four feet away, he couldn't make out the features on Isabel's face.

"It's…true… Jason." Her voice, drenched in fear, faltered.

"Back away…now," said the man covered in shadows. He was dressed in black, which made him even harder to see.

Heart raging against his rib cage, sweat trickling down his neck, Jason took a step back even as he tried to come up with a way to overtake the man holding Isabel.

Isabel's frantic breathing seemed augmented in the darkness and silence of the library. Dragging Isabel with him, the man slipped toward a dark corner of the room.

There was a brief burst of light as a door opened and the man pulled Isabel through. The door shut and he heard a clicking sound. Footsteps retreating downstairs. Jason raced toward it. Locked. This was an exit the Bureau hadn't accounted for.

He ran to the window that was on the same side of the room as the door. Down below, he saw Isabel being dragged toward a black truck that was parked off away from the other vehicles. From that side of the property, there was only one road out.

He hurried down the stairs toward his own car, praying that he would be able to get to Isabel in time. He sprinted through the back part of the main floor. The noise of the partygoers dimmed as he went through a part of the house where there weren't many people, only some of the hired help. There was no time to alert the agent on the premises. Isabel's life depended on his getting out to that road as fast as he could.

As he ran toward his car, the momentary image of Isabel's terrified expression when the light had come through the open door bombarded his thoughts.

Jumping into his loaner car, he shifted into gear. He could see the black truck winding its way up the road. He pressed the gas. His car swerved, but he straightened it out. Conditions were far from ideal.

Shadow man's truck disappeared around a corner. Jason prayed he would be able to get to Isabel before it was too late.

Isabel gripped the steering wheel as she struggled to take in air, to remain calm. She'd seen Jason's car behind them for just a moment on the straight part of the road. She slowed as they rounded the curve, hoping Jason would be able to keep up.

"Drive faster," said the man with the gun.

She glanced over at him.

He grinned, showing all his teeth. "Thought I'd never see you again, Isabel."

Nick Solomon. The last person on earth she wanted to see. "I heard you got out of prison." He must be connected with the smuggling ring. How else would he have known she was in the library?

"You've been following my exploits, have you?"

She had paid attention to his release date because she wanted to avoid him. "I thought I heard you went down to California."

"I did for a while, Blondie." He scooted closer, still holding the gun on her. "Let's just say a much more lucrative opportunity came up here in Silver Strike."

Nick instructed her to take several more turns. She wasn't familiar with this road. She checked the rearview mirror.

"I think we lost your little partner there. I don't know why you're with him, anyway. If you wanted to get back into the life, if the word on the street is true, you should have called me."

She pressed her teeth together. As much as she wanted to tell Nick she had changed and the last thing she wanted was a life of crime, she swallowed her words. The smuggling ring believed she wanted in on their action, and she had to continue that ruse. "I'm happy with my current partner."

"What's his name, anyway?"

So they hadn't been able to identify Jason. That was why they'd communicated with her.

"Decided to go all quiet on me, huh?" He sat back in the seat, staring at her in a way that put her even more on edge. They drove for at least twenty minutes. He waved the gun in the air. "Turn that way and park when you see the little cabins."

She turned onto a long unplowed driveway where there were several cabins and a larger lodge. This was probably a church camp that was only used in the summer.

"Stop before the truck gets stuck."

She pressed the brakes. Nick held out his hands for the keys. They were miles from anything or anyone. They had encountered no other traffic on the road or passed any houses.

She slammed the keys into his clammy palm.

Her clutch rested on the seat. Nick shoved it into her stomach. "I assume the item of interest is in there. Give it to me."

Her hands were shaking as she undid the clasp. "This is what you were supposed to get back for your boss, right? What good am I to you? Why complicate things?"

Again, the toothy smile. "I have plans for you, my dear."

His words were like mercury in her veins, spreading a deadly poison through her.

She pulled the bookmark from the purse, unfolded the protective case it was in and showed him.

"Very nice."

What had she ever seen in this man? She was sixteen when she met him. Her mother had had a string of boyfriends. She'd never known her father. Nick had paid attention to her at first, told her she was pretty, bought her gifts, given her the affection she'd craved.

He pointed the gun at her. "Get out of the truck and go over to the stone building."

She opened the truck door. Wind blew the snow around. Cold settled on her bare skin. Her ball gown had gotten ripped in the struggle. Her exposed arms were goose pimpled from the cold.

Nick trudged behind her, still holding the gun on her. "I have to say. You look so beautiful tonight. When I saw you, it made me think of old times. We could have been something for each other."

Isabel paused midstride briefly but didn't respond. Fear made it almost impossible for her to speak anyway. What was he planning?

The door to the large stone lodge had a lock and chain on it that had been cut.

"Go inside," Nick urged.

She pushed open the door. The main meeting area had a few benches and a large fireplace.

Without a coat, Isabel was shivering.

"Do you like it here? It's my home away from home. Why don't you build us a nice romantic fire?"

She pressed her lips together, fighting back the words she wanted to say. How he had ruined her life. How she wanted nothing to do with him or the people he associated with.

He pulled out a phone and stepped over to a corner of the room, still watching her and holding the gun.

Wood and kindling were stacked by the fire.

Nick blocked the door, so there was no way for her to escape. Besides, he had the truck keys. She wouldn't get far in the cold, not dressed the way she was.

She struck a match to the kindling she had stacked in the grate and tossed in more paper. Flames blackened and ate the paper and tiny pieces of wood.

Though Nick was speaking in a low tone, she gathered enough of the conversation to discern that he was talking to someone about the bookmark. At one point, he patted his chest where he'd placed it.

The fire increased in intensity, and she threw on a small log. She held her hands out to the warmth and then rubbed her arms.

Nick finished his phone call and strode toward her. The look in his eyes turned her stomach.

She rubbed her palms over her arms. "I'm really cold. Can I see if I can find a sweater or something around here?"

"I could keep you warm." Again, that sick smile.

Repulsed, she took a step back. "I think I'll try to find a coat or blanket. Maybe some kid left something behind." She turned, looking for a door that might lead to storage or a closet.

She stepped across the room, swung a door open and found board games and outdoor equipment. A sweatshirt heaped in a box on the floor. She grabbed it, assessed it to be a few sizes too big and put it on. It hung down past her waist.

When she turned around, Nick was watching her. He'd put the gun away in his coat. "You sure looked beautiful tonight. You even look cute with that sweatshirt on. What do you say—join me? This isn't small-time. We could make a fortune."

She was struck by how pathetic and desperate he sounded. So that was why he'd dragged her here. He thought he could talk her into being with him.

She shook her head. "I just want to go home, please."

"Come on, Isabel. Don't you want to be rich? This isn't petty stuff for me. I'm connected all the way to the top."

Her senses went on high alert. Was he telling the truth? Did Nick know who was behind the smuggling, or was he just bragging to try to win her back?

He blocked the door so she couldn't step back out into the main room. She had to play this thing to the end. "I'm happy with the arrangement I have."

Rage flared in his eyes and he reached out and grabbed her. "You were meant to be with me." His hands closed around her wrists.

"Nick, please, you're hurting me." She struggled to get away.

He pressed toward her trying to kiss her. She kicked him hard in the shins so he doubled over and got out of her way. She ran toward the door.

Nick was just recovering when she swung the door open and ran outside. She raced toward one of the far cabins hidden in the trees. The snow was of a soft enough texture that she hadn't left clear footprints. She was glad she'd chosen to wear boots with her dress. At least her feet were warm. He'd find her sooner or later, though. Though she'd gained access to the cabin, she needed to come up with an escape plan.

What could she do? Run to the truck and lock all the doors until he agreed to take her home? No, he would never do that. She could file kidnapping charges against him.

She took out her cell phone. She could tell Jason where she was.

She heard Nick moving through the camp, opening and shutting the cabin doors. No time to make the call.

She slipped out the back door of the cabin and hid behind a tree. His footsteps reached her ears.

"Come on out, Isabel." He sounded almost whiny. "It can be like old times. You and me."

She took in a breath, willing her heart to slow down. The only way off this mountain without blowing her cover was to play along. She'd make Nick think she was interested in getting back with him. Acid rose up from her stomach at the thought of having to pretend to like him.

She stepped out, prepared to call to Nick, when a hand went over her mouth.

ELEVEN

For the second time since they'd met, Jason had to subdue Isabel into silence by putting a hand over her mouth. This time, she must have sensed it was him because she stopped struggling right away.

"I've got the car down the road," Jason whispered.

Nick cried out. "Isabel. Blondie." He shone the flashlight in her direction. Both of them got caught in the light just as they turned to run.

Isabel scrambled down the snowy hill, slowed by her dress. When she looked over her shoulder, the flashlight was moving away from them. Nick was probably going to get his truck so he could chase them.

Jason jumped into the car and revved the engine. She swung the passenger-side door open and scooted in beside him, snapping her seat belt on.

"How did you find me?"

"I saw the smoke from the chimney." He pressed the accelerator and burst forward on the snow-covered road. "When I lost you, I called our friends at the Bureau. Couple agents are out looking for you." Affection and relief collided inside him. "I'm glad I'm the one who found you."

"Me too." Nuances of affection permeated her words. Isabel brushed a stray strand of hair off her face. When he thought he'd lost her at the party, he'd felt a chasm inside him he didn't understand.

"Nice outfit." Even after all she'd been through, she looked beautiful.

She stared down at the sweatshirt. "It's what all the divas are wearing these days."

He caught the levity in her voice, grateful that she could have a sense of humor even while they were still in danger. The guy who had taken her was bound to come after them.

"What's that guy's game, anyway? Why didn't he just take the bookmark?"

"Let's just say he's someone I would rather not associate with."

"But he knows you?"

"He's the reason I have a record." Her voice dropped half an octave and she turned slightly away from him.

Jason knew from what the Bureau had told

him that Isabel's old boyfriend was named Nick Solomon. "The past is in the past." He hoped his words communicated that he still believed in her.

Headlights loomed behind them.

Jason stared in the rearview mirror. "Didn't take him long to catch up."

Nick closed the distance between the two vehicles.

Jason pressed the accelerator, feeling a surge of excitement in his veins. Danger did that for him. But he had Isabel to think of now. He needed to get her to a safe place.

Both vehicles slipped on the icy road.

Isabel braced an arm on the dashboard.

Jason righted the car and watched the speedometer nudge toward forty, a dangerous speed in these conditions. Nick was right on his bumper.

They entered a section of the road that was switchback curves. Jason stayed close to the inside as he maneuvered the car around the tight turns.

Nick tapped their bumper. Their car lurched. Jason gripped the wheel, bringing the car back under control.

Headlights filled the rearview mirror. "Hold on." Jason pressed the accelerator to the floor.

Nick's headlights got smaller.

"I think we're going too fast," Isabel said breathlessly as her hand clasped the armrest.

"We just need to put a little distance between us," Jason said.

Visibility was reduced in the darkness. A curve came up without warning. The car slid sideways. Jason turned the wheel in the direction of the skid, hoping to straighten the car.

They continued to slide. The car came to a stop. The engine had quit. Jason turned the key in the ignition.

Nick's truck barreled toward them, ramming them in the side by the back door. The whole car shook.

Jason tried to start the car again and the motor revved to life. Nick backed up, preparing to ram them again. Illumination from Nick's headlights filled the car, making it hard to see.

"He's trying to push us in the ditch." Isabel's voice filled with terror.

"Not if I can help it." Jason pressed the gas. The back wheels spun.

Nick's truck loomed toward them a second time. He rammed them hard enough that the car slid down the hillside and then tilted on its side. Metal creaked and groaned.

The driver's side of the car was closest to the ground. "Crawl out," Jason said as he unbuckled his seat belt.

He heard Isabel struggling in the darkness. "I can't get the door open. It's too heavy."

"Out the back, then." Nick was probably waiting for them. "Let me go first." He crawled through the car and pushed open the back hatch. His feet touched the snowy ground, and he reached a hand out for Isabel.

About fifteen feet above them, Nick's headlights glared down at them. He didn't see Nick anywhere.

Isabel wasn't dressed for running in the snow, but it was the only choice they had. If they could escape Nick's clutches, Jason could call for help. The other agents out looking for Isabel were in the area.

They took off running as gunshots exploded close to their feet.

Jason ran blindly, unable to make out what was in front of them. Isabel stumbled. He helped her to her feet. He heard footsteps behind them but saw no light.

They came to a cluster of evergreens. Jason and Isabel wove through them while Nick's footfalls seemed to surround them. If Jason could just get to a hiding place... Isabel's dress made swishing noises as they ran that could give them away.

He came to a spot where the trees were clustered close together and pulled her behind a tree with a thick trunk. Isabel's back was pressed against the tree and he stood facing her. Their breathing seemed augmented by the darkness and the silence.

Nick's footsteps drew near, slowed, stopped altogether.

Jason held his breath.

The footfalls were slower but very near. Nick seemed to be doing a circle around them, stopping every four or five steps.

As close as Jason was standing to Isabel, he could sense her body tensing.

Finally, the footfalls retreated and then faded in the distance. That didn't mean he wouldn't turn around and come back.

Jason pulled out his phone, praying he would get a signal. He stared at the screen. Nothing.

Isabel gripped his arm just above the elbow. "We can get back up the hill and take Nick's truck."

"Yes. Good." He took off running with Isabel right behind him. Had Nick doubled back or had he gone deeper into the trees? There was no way to know.

They scrambled up the hill. Her hand slipped into his as he pushed toward the top. Isabel had no gloves. Her hands were probably icicles by now. They ran past their overturned car.

Nick's headlights were no longer on. If Nick

had taken the keys, Jason knew how to hot-wire a car, but it would cost them precious seconds.

Isabel hurried around to the passenger side of the truck. Jason reached for the handle of the driver's-side door. Cold metal pressed into his temple.

"I think someone here needs to die tonight." Nick's voice was menacing.

"No," Isabel shouted from the other side of the truck. She hurried around to face the two men. "You don't want to do that, Nick. You'll go back to prison."

"You should be with me, Isabel. You're my soul mate."

"You don't have to kill him." The silence surrounded them like a heavy blanket.

Nick pressed the gun barrel deeper into Jason's temple.

"Leave him out here in the cold. He'll freeze. Then you won't be charged with his death." Isabel took a step toward the two men.

"He deserves to die," Nick said.

"No, Nick. I'll go with you. You're right—we were meant to be together. But just leave him here. He won't make it back."

The pressure of the gun let up a little on Jason's skin.

"You'll go with me?"

"Yes."

What was she saying? This guy was a nutjob. How could she sacrifice her life like this? Or did she have something else in mind?

Nick pushed on Jason's back. "Get down the hill by your wrecked car. Don't try anything."

Jason took a step. Nick held the gun on him. Jason brushed by Isabel. In the darkness, she reached out, touching his fingers only briefly. Was that her way of saying she was going to be okay, she had a plan, or was it just a goodbye?

He turned, thinking he could grab her. They could run again.

She shook her head.

"Keep moving!" Nick shouted.

He had to fight for her. He wasn't about to give up so easily. He reached out for her arm, prepared to run.

"Jason, no."

A gunshot cracked the air around him. He felt a stinging sensation on his upper arm. He'd been grazed by a bullet.

"The next one goes straight through your heart," Nick said.

"It will be okay, Jason. This is what I want. I want to be with Nick." Agitation colored every syllable she uttered.

His heart squeezed down to the size of a walnut as an invisible weight pressed on his chest.

She was putting herself in so much danger…to save him, to help the investigation?

"Please," she said, her voice barely above a whisper.

Jason made his way down the hill and stood beside the overturned car.

"Now lie down on the ground on your stomach and don't move until we're gone."

Jason's hands curled into tight fists. He really hated this guy.

He lay down in the snow, a chill seeping through his layers of clothes. He squeezed his eyes shut, listening to truck doors slamming and an engine fading into the distance in the cold dark night.

What had he allowed to happen? He rose to his feet, vowing to rescue Isabel before it was too late.

Once again, Nick had forced Isabel to sit behind the wheel, pointing the gun at her.

"If we're going to be partners, don't you think you should quit pointing that thing at me?"

Nick leaned close and brushed a finger down her cheek. "You got to prove yourself to me. Show your loyalty, Blondie."

She steeled herself against his touch, not giving away how much he repulsed her.

For a moment, she listened to the sound of the

car's tires rolling over packed snow. She stared out into the lonely dark night.

Nick would have killed Jason. She knew that much. Her life was only at risk if he figured out she was undercover or if his rage got out of control. She had to choose her moves carefully.

Jason had a cell phone. If he could get to a place where he had a signal, he'd be picked up. The other agents might even find him. She had to trust his survival skills. He'd be all right.

Somehow, she'd have to find a way to communicate with Jason. Nick had taken her phone. He'd hinted he knew who was behind the smuggling operation. This was the connection they needed to take this thing apart.

Saving Jason's life had been only part of the reason she'd made the choice she had. What she wanted even more than to help the investigation was to see to it that Nick Solomon went to prison for a long time.

Nick leaned so close to her she could feel his hot breath on her cheek.

"Show my loyalty? What do you want me to do, Nick?"

"There's a pickup tonight at a property Sun and Ski manages. The cabin on Old Fort Road."

"Yes, I know it." She took in a breath to steady her nerves as she stared out at the road ahead. "What time?"

"Midnight. We'll have time to go to your place so you can change into something that isn't so noisy."

Her neck muscles tensed. The ball had started at eight. Midnight had to be maybe an hour from now. How was she going to get in touch with Jason before then? Nick would watch her like a hawk.

He leaned back in the seat and chuckled. "You play this right, and it could be the start of a great partnership." He kissed her cheek. "In so many ways."

"Yes, indeed."

He patted her hand. "You're looking forward to it, aren't you, Blondie?"

She cringed. She hated being called Blondie. "Of course I am, Nick. You and me, just like old times."

"You have an in with Sun and Ski, so no more having to fish out the entry codes."

At least now she knew her boss wasn't involved. "What do you mean fish out the entry codes?"

Any information she could garner would be helpful.

"What do you care?" Suspicion clouded his words, and she feared she'd overplayed her hand.

Nick kept the gun pointed at her as she came

to the edge of town and made several turns to get to the Sun and Ski office.

As they approached the building, Nick sat up straighter. He looked from side to side, homing in on the dark cars parked on the street. He waved the gun in the air. "Go past. Keep driving."

The Bureau probably was watching the office and her home.

She checked the rearview mirror by raising her eyes but not moving her head. Just as she turned onto another street, headlights came on at the end of the street opposite the Sun and Ski office.

Nick instructed her where to turn until they came to a trailer park on the outskirts of town. They pulled up to one of the trailers where the lights were still on and a television glowed through the window. She'd been here before when she dated Nick.

"Go in and get a pair of black pants and a shirt from Aunt Phoebe's closet. Hurry." He lifted the gun slightly. "Don't try anything."

She met his gaze. "You know I wouldn't, Nick." Her voice had sounded a little too forceful. She remembered Aunt Phoebe from when she had dated Nick all those years ago. Chances were she was passed out on the couch with her two cats.

Isabel stepped inside the dimly lit trailer.

True to form, Aunt Phoebe snored away in an easy chair. There was only one cat resting on her lap, though.

Isabel saw no landline or cell anywhere in the living room. She hurried down the hallway to where the bedroom was. As she grabbed a black shirt and pants from a drawer, she glanced around, searching for a cell phone.

She spied it on the bureau beside Aunt Phoebe's bed. She slipped into the shirt and zipped up the pants. Phoebe was maybe a size bigger than Isabel. She'd stepped toward the bureau when Nick's voice pelted her back.

"You'll need a coat too." He held up a ratty-looking dark blue ski jacket, then stepped toward her and kissed her on the lips.

Everything in her wanted to push him away, but she planted her feet and let him kiss her as she went cold as a stone on the inside. She stepped back. "We better hurry, don't you think?"

Nick squeezed her upper arm. "Let's do this, baby."

He made her drive up to the cabin. She focused on the tiny bit of road illuminated by the headlights. Now was her opportunity to try to get as much information as she could.

"Why does the guy in charge pick these vacation homes for the drop-off and pickup? There has to be an easier way to do the smuggling."

Nick chuckled. "I think he likes the game of it. Breaking into rich people's fancy digs. He likes the idea of people coming into their homes and feeling like something is off but not being able to say why."

The guy behind this was a little twisted psychologically. She drove on in silence for a few more minutes. She had to choose her words carefully to not give herself away. She knew from experience that Nick could spin out of control if he felt betrayed. "He told you that?"

"Yeah. One night when we'd had too much to drink." Nick shook his head.

So Nick hadn't been bragging about being close to the top in this whole operation.

"I gotta hand it to you, Nick. I'm impressed. Word on the street is that millions in merchandise changes hands."

The flattery changed Nick's whole demeanor. He sat back in his seat, lowered the gun and tilted his head toward the ceiling. "I'm telling you, Isabel, this is the big time. I think I might be able to take over this whole operation."

Nick had always had an overblown view of his criminal skills.

She had a hundred other questions she wanted to ask him, but she needed to bide her time.

The road curved around several more times.

Nick sat up straight and peered out his window, suddenly alert.

Her heart squeezed tight. "What is it?"

She hadn't seen any headlights behind her since they'd left town. She couldn't assume Jason had made it to safety and been able to alert the agents, though she prayed that was the case.

Nick twisted from side to side, clearly nervous. Now she remembered how mercurial his moods could be. When she was with him as a teenager, it was like the ground was always shifting beneath her feet. "What's that helicopter doing out here?"

Was it possible the FBI had decided a helicopter was a better choice in tracking them on this remote road? "The resort does rides, remember?"

"Yeah, but at night?" He curled his hands into fists and pounded one against the other.

"Maybe. I don't know," she said.

Nick slammed the back of his head against the seat and stared at the ceiling.

"It's probably just a private citizen. Lots of people own helicopters around here." She struggled to keep her voice neutral. His volcanic personality affected her even now. "I think we should go forward with the plan. You don't want your boss upset with you, right?"

Tension invaded the car like a lead blanket.

Nick continued to stare at the ceiling. He let out a heavy breath. "Are you ordering me around, Is…a…bel?" He dragged out her name as his voice filled with accusation.

Sweat trickled down the back of her neck. To hide the fear in her voice, she enunciated each word with care. "I. Would. Never. Do. That."

The cabin came into view. The car rolled toward it as Isabel tried to calm her nerves with a deep breath.

Nick peered out the window again. "The chopper is off that way."

She stopped the car, turned off the ignition and waited for Nick to tell her what to do.

Unbuckling his seat belt, he turned to face her. He waited for a long moment before saying anything, probably because he knew the silence would make her even more afraid. "You sure ask a lot of questions, Isabel."

Whatever suspicion he'd had about the helicopter was now being transferred to her.

"I'm just curious about your life, Nick. We have a lot of catching up to do."

The answer seemed to satisfy him. "You know the code for this house?"

"Yes."

"You can get more codes, right?"

"Well, I—"

"It would really help me look good to the boss."

"Sure, Nick." She wasn't about to hurt Sun and Ski's reputation in that way, but for now, to keep Nick on an even keel, she would agree to anything he said.

"You'll be picking up five silver coins sitting in a dish on the entryway table. Don't turn on any lights. You know the layout of the place, right?"

"Yes."

He leaned toward her and kissed her on the cheek, then placed a leather pouch in her hand. "Put the coins in here." He let out a yelp. "This is the big time for you and me."

Her cheek felt slimy where he'd kissed it, but she didn't wipe it away. Nick Solomon was a bad man, and she would do whatever it took to see he went to jail.

"Okay, I'm ready to do this," she said. Her voice didn't even sound like her own, all light and airy. Anything to not make Nick fly off the handle again.

"You do good tonight, and I'll let you do the meet-up with the buyer."

She pushed open the door, zipped up the old coat against the nighttime chill and hurried toward the house. Her heart pounded against her rib cage, and her fingers trembled as she touched the keypad and slipped into the dark house.

Maybe that helicopter had been the Bureau's. All she knew was that right now she was on her own. She'd be all right if she could keep Nick from erupting. He was paranoid. After this was all over, he'd probably stay close to her or demand that she check in with him every hour.

She felt around on the table until her fingers touched the bowl. She scooped up the coins and put them in the leather pouch Nick had given her. She'd unearthed some valuable information, and she prayed Jason had made it to safety so she could find a way to communicate with him.

TWELVE

Tension threaded through Jason's torso as he watched the glaring taillights of Nick Solomon's truck.

Through the use of a chopper, the Bureau had alerted him to their position. He'd slipped in to tail Nick's truck as soon as they were close to town. From the outside, it looked like Isabel had switched loyalties back to her old boyfriend. From the chatter on the radio, that was what the Bureau thought. He knew otherwise. Back on that remote road, Isabel had saved his life.

When she left him, it had taken him less than half an hour to get picked up by one of the agents. The Bureau had scrambled to put moving surveillance on Nick and Isabel.

Now it was his job to get to Isabel and have her explain herself to the agents in charge.

Nick's truck came to a stop outside the Sun and Ski office on the opposite side of the street.

Jason turned his own car up an alley and killed the lights. He slipped out onto the street.

Isabel and Nick got out of the car. She handed him something and he gave her a hug.

A twinge of doubt played at the corners of Jason's mind. She sure hugged him like she cared about him. Maybe Jason just didn't like the idea of her hugging anyone. He was starting to have feelings for her.

Isabel crossed the street. Nick got back in the truck but didn't drive away. So that was his game. He was going to watch her all night.

Jason slipped around to the back of the building. The offices were dark. Even if they didn't lock up during the day, they must lock the place at night. The window of Isabel's little apartment looked like the old-fashioned kind that would swing open if it wasn't latched. He climbed on top of a Dumpster that was just beneath the window. He shimmied up a pipe and hooked his hands onto the windowsill.

He hung there for a moment wondering if he'd made a mistake. The rough texture of the brick wall provided him with enough traction to push with his feet until his hand touched the bottom of the window.

He pushed on the window. It didn't budge.

He heard footsteps in the alley.

Jason tried to pull himself up but felt his

arms straining against his weight. He was going to fall on the hard metal of the Dumpster, or worse—onto the concrete below.

The footsteps grew louder. No one else would be up at this hour. That had to be Nick doing some sort of patrol around the building.

He was about ready to let go and make a run for it when the window swung open and hands wrapped around his wrists. Isabel pulled him through the window. They sat on the floor in the dark.

"Stay low. He's out there."

"I know. I stayed on the couch so I could watch him through the front window. I saw him leave his truck," she said.

The window above them was still open. Would that be a red flag to Nick?

He held his breath, tuning his ears to the sounds outside. The footsteps moved past and then faded.

Isabel's hand slipped over the top of his. "I'm glad you made it out. I was afraid I'd made the wrong decision."

Her hand felt warm and silky smooth on top of his.

He leaned close to her and whispered, "You saved my life. I'm pretty sure he would have killed me."

Warmth like a down comforter seemed to

surround them as they sat very close together, their shoulders touching. It felt good to be this close to her, as if he'd known her all his life.

A long moment passed before Isabel spoke.

"I wasn't sure if it would work, but I thought I might find something out if I went with Nick."

"That was a risk. He's clearly unstable."

"I can handle him." Her voice wavered a little.

She'd been afraid, but she'd gone with Nick anyway. He admired her bravery. He turned to face her. "You've got some explaining to do to the agents in charge. They think you've gone rogue, but I never believed it for a minute."

Her face was very close to his, their noses almost touching. She reached up and brushed her finger over his cheek. Her touch sent a charge of electricity through him.

"Thank you for believing in me," she whispered.

Her voice reminded him of a mountain stream or a cool summer morning.

"What did you find out?"

"Nick knows who the kingpin is. He's in contact with him."

"That's huge."

"He's going to let me join in on the buyer pickup for the coins we took from the cabin."

"Isabel, there is risk involved with doing all this." The thought of her being in danger, of having to deal with the volatile Nick, made his chest tight.

"I know that. I'm willing to do it if Nick Solomon goes to jail for a long time."

He detected the resolve in her voice. Isabel had pushed the investigation further than anyone. Still, he didn't like her going into the line of fire again. "We need to talk to the Bureau. Tell them what you found out. See what they say."

"Nick will be watching me day and night. He's paranoid anyway, and I don't think he is totally convinced I'm on his side. I'm sure he'll come in and check on me first thing in the morning before I go to work. It was hard enough to convince him not to come into the apartment to guard me. Can I talk to them over the phone?"

"Michael will want to talk to you in person. They have this thing about reading body language and all that. I'll sneak you out tonight. You'll talk to Michael. We'll bring you back before first light so you can get some sleep."

"We can slip out the back. I have a rope ladder in case there is ever a fire." She burst to her feet and hurried down the hallway in the dark.

It would be a risk to even turn on lights.

Still crawling, Jason made his way into the living room. Light from the street shone in.

Nick's car was now parked on this side of the street. He couldn't discern if Nick was in the car or not.

Isabel whispered from the corner of the living room. "I've got it."

He'd moved back toward the window when there was a knock on the door.

"Isabel, it's me. I need to see you." Nick's voice was filled with that nauseating whiny quality.

Isabel tossed the ladder toward Jason.

"Nick, I'm trying to get some sleep here." Her voice sounded groggy. "You'll see me in the morning just like I promised."

"Come on, Isabel. Just for a minute. Just give me a little hug. I need to see you, baby."

Jason scooted down the hallway and hung the ladder out the window, feeling his muscles knot up with tension. Why couldn't that creep leave her alone?

Come on, Isabel—don't open that door.

"Nick, I'm just really tired."

"Come on, baby. I'm out in that cold car." The intensity of his voice changed, becoming less pleading and darker. "Open the door, Isabel."

He heard the door handle rattling.

Jason craned his neck to see Isabel standing by the door. He wanted to run down the hallway, swing the door open and punch Nick in the face. The only thing that stopped him was that he knew it would put Isabel at risk in an even bigger way.

"Nick, I'm going back to bed. You should do the same." After placing a chair underneath the locked door, she stomped through the living room. "Good night." She opened and shut the bedroom door without going in.

Jason barely heard her footsteps as she scurried to join him in the hallway.

Nick continued to bang on the door and plead.

"We should go now before he gets back to his car," Isabel said.

"What if he breaks in and finds you're not here?" said Jason.

"That lock is pretty solid and I put the chair there."

The banging stopped and footfalls sounded on the stairs that led down to the street. Nick had given up.

Isabel burst to her feet, pushed the window open wider and swung her leg over the sill. Their plan was fraught with risk if Nick caught them. But the Bureau's coming here would be just as dangerous as long as Nick was watching and running patrols.

Heart pounding, Jason peered out the window. Isabel was halfway down. What if Nick decided to do another circle around the building?

Hearing her feet hit the concrete, he crawled out.

She shout-whispered up at him. "Make sure the window is closed."

After closing the window, he crawled down, struggled a little to disengage the ladder and then hid it in the Dumpster, so there would be no evidence of their escape. How they would get her back in unnoticed was a problem he'd solve later.

He led her around to the alley where he'd parked his car. Her hand found his in the darkness. He squeezed her fingers as warmth from her touch spread through him.

Here they were, inches from danger, slipping through the darkness, and the thought that was foremost in his mind was how much he liked being with her.

They got into the car. Jason started the engine but didn't turn on the lights. A truck blocked the alley up ahead. He'd have to back out onto the street where Nick was parked.

He clicked the lights on, reasoning that that would look less suspicious, then backed onto the street and rolled forward.

Isabel stayed low in the seat but craned her neck to watch Nick's truck. "He's not moving."

Jason phoned Michael, and they agreed to meet at an all-night coffee shop. He drove through the empty streets. Falling snow made the streetlights seem murky. They encountered only a little bit of traffic. A car slipped in behind them and followed them for several blocks but didn't pull into the coffee shop.

When they entered the coffee shop, there was a group of twentysomething people dressed in ski gear. Cars in the parking lot had been loaded down with snowboards and skis. They must have been gearing up for some early-morning skiing. The group of three women and four men joked and laughed as they drank their hot beverages.

A woman with a laptop in front of her was the only other patron besides Michael and the skiers. Michael's hair was disheveled and he had an overall droopy appearance despite the crisp white shirt and slacks he wore. A steaming mug sat on the table in front of him.

Jason and Isabel both ordered herbal tea. They took their warm mugs over to where Michael waited. Isabel scooted into the booth opposite Michael.

"Isabel has some important information."

After squeezing her shoulder, Jason sat down in the booth beside her.

Isabel cleared her throat. "Nick Solomon knows the man behind all of this."

Michael sat up straighter. Light seemed to come into his eyes.

"He's invited me to go with him for the buyer pickup. I think he's testing my loyalty."

"I think it's too risky," Jason said.

Michael smiled at Isabel. "You've pushed this investigation over the top. We might be able to wrap things up." Michael couldn't hide the excitement in his voice.

Maybe the investigation had been the most important thing to Jason at one point, but now he just wanted Isabel to be safe and away from that nutjob Nick.

"There's something else," said Isabel. "Nick says that the reason the guy does the pickups in empty vacation homes is to stick it to rich people to make them feel uneasy in their own homes."

Michael nodded slowly. "That might be something our profiler could use." He looked directly at Isabel. "We could provide you with protection for the buyer pickup."

Jason opened his mouth to protest.

"I'll do it if you promise me Nick Solomon goes to jail when this investigation is all over."

"We can manage that," Michael said.

That was a promise they might not be able to keep. What if Nick ran off or slipped through their clutches in some other way? Michael was so fixated on catching the kingpin, he wasn't being realistic with Isabel.

"I'll do it, then, and keep up my cover until you catch the guy and charge Nick."

Jason leaned forward. "I want to be there as part of the protection team." If he couldn't stop Isabel, at least he could see to it she was safe.

Michael nodded. "When is the buyer exchange?"

"Tomorrow night. Nick will let me know when and where, probably at the last minute."

"He's watching her pretty closely. I need to get her back to her place before first light," said Jason.

"Once Nick tells me the when and where of the buyer meet-up, I might not be able to let you know."

"Leave that to us. We'll stay close to you, Isabel. You might not see us, but know that we are watching," Michael said.

Isabel nodded. "I'm ready to do this."

Underneath the soft lights of the coffee shop, her skin appeared smooth as porcelain and her cheeks had a rosy glow. Maybe she was afraid, but the intensity of her features, the determination he saw in her eyes, did not give that fear away. What courage.

"We'll get a man to tail you within a few hours. And we'll have someone watching Nick." Michael looked at Jason. "You stay close until we can get that in place."

Jason nodded.

They said their goodbyes, and Jason and Isabel returned to his car. They drove across town, not seeing a single car.

"Are you sure you want to do this?"

"Yes. Don't try to talk me out of it," she said.

That was that. He drove on in silence. When they were a block away from Isabel's place, he saw that Nick's car was no longer parked on the street. He circled the block and drove up the alley to make sure Nick hadn't parked somewhere else.

"He must have given up and gone home for some sleep," Isabel said.

They couldn't get in through the door because of the chair Isabel had put in place. He helped her through the window by standing on the Dumpster and boosting her up.

When she'd pulled herself through the window, she turned around and looked down at him. "Thank you, Jason, for everything." The moonlight brought out the softness of her features. He felt a surge of deep affection for her that went beyond admiration for her bravery.

Several times he drove the car around the block to see if Nick had returned before settling in his car in the back parking lot. He slept in short spurts through the night. Toward morning, he stared up at the window where he'd last seen Isabel and prayed they weren't making a mistake letting her go through with this.

THIRTEEN

Isabel awoke feeling like her heart was in a vise. She squeezed her eyes shut, touched her palm to her beating heart and prayed that God would give her the strength and courage to face this day and what she had to do.

When she looked out her back window, Jason's car was not in the parking lot. Of course, he needed to go home and get some sleep. She stepped into the living room. A sense of dread filled her when she saw Nick's car parked out front again. She stared at it and took in a deep breath to clear her head. One of the other cars on the street must be the FBI guy.

Once she checked in with Mary and got her marching orders for the day, she stepped outside, where Nick waited for her.

He offered her a crooked grin with lots of teeth in it. "Thought I'd tag along while you did your work."

Nick drove her while she picked up groceries

and flowers and got two houses ready. All day long, she sensed that they were being followed and watched. Though when she glanced around or checked her rearview mirror, she could never spot the tail. She just had to trust what Michael had promised. Toward evening, Nick suggested they have dinner together. He hadn't said anything about the buyer pickup all day.

The restaurant was one of the more expensive in town with soft lighting and a hushed atmosphere.

"Go ahead—order the most expensive thing on the menu," Nick said.

Her stomach was so tied in knots she doubted she could swallow a pea. "Think I'll just get a salad."

He gritted his teeth and narrowed his eyes at her. "I said order the most expensive thing on the menu."

She wasn't sure how much more of his controlling behavior she could take. She glanced around the restaurant, wondering which of the patrons was her protection. She noticed Larry, the man with the graying temples who had picked Jason and her up after they got away from the Wilson house.

A man two tables over lowered his menu. Jason winked at her and put the menu back up to cover his face. The exchange sent a spark of light through her.

She turned her attention back toward Nick. "Okay, I'll get something besides salad."

"Now, that's my Isabel. Thank you for dropping the bad attitude," Nick said. His phone rang. He checked the number and a shadow seemed to fall over his face. "I have to take this." He got up and stepped toward the men's restroom, speaking in low tones.

Jason dropped his menu again and made a face at Isabel.

She wanted to laugh out loud.

The waiter was approaching their table just as Nick burst into the dining room, clearly agitated. "Come on—we're going."

She looked at the waiter. Jason covered his face with the menu again. "But we haven't ordered yet."

Nick squeezed her arm so tight it hurt. "I said we're going."

She got up as Nick pulled her through the restaurant. Jason was no longer at the table where he'd been watching.

A light snow twirled out of the sky as Nick dragged her through the parking lot, yanked the door open and pushed her toward his truck.

"What's going on?" Her heart was beating a mile a minute.

"We're going to the buyer pickup." Nick glanced from side to side, surveying the parking lot. "Get in the truck."

She climbed in. Nick got behind the wheel and sped out of the parking lot. She didn't dare look around to see if her protection was there and give herself away. She had to trust that they would be. Seeing Jason, knowing that he was close, eased her fear.

The streets of Silver Strike were bustling with activity. The winter music festival had brought additional tourists and weekenders.

A light turned red before Nick could get through. He cursed at the traffic and slammed his hand on the steering wheel.

His agitation made her stomach churn. Maybe a buyer pickup made him nervous, but this felt over the top. His mood had changed after the phone call. Traffic remained heavy even once they got out on the highway.

She glanced up at the rearview mirror without moving her head. Several cars were behind them. She struggled to take a deep breath.

He took the exit that led to the venue for the music festival.

"Why here?"

The parking lot for the festival was filled with people.

"Public places are best." He adjusted his hands on the wheel and stared straight ahead.

Nick found a parking space after cursing out several other drivers. He was out of the truck and on Isabel's side of the truck just as she pushed the door open. He grabbed her sleeve and pulled her toward the venue, which was at the base of the ski hill. Inside, a band was just taking the stage. The venue had a large open floor with high-top tables around the edges and a bar and grill at the far end of the concert hall.

Nick manacled his hand around her wrist and pulled her through the thick crowd. How was he going to find a buyer among all these people? She glanced around at the concertgoers. For a moment, she thought she had spotted Jason, but then the face disappeared in the crowd.

The band struck up an intense blues number that pummeled her ears. People pressed on her from all sides as they squeezed through the bodies. Nick held her wrist so tight it hurt. She wanted to pull free and run.

But she needed to stick with the plan, play her part and meet this buyer. He got to a wall and led her up some stairs into a private box for viewing the concert. The room had several leather couches.

Nick closed the window, muffling the noise of the concert.

"This is where we're meeting the buyer?"

"Yeah." He shoved his hands in his pockets and didn't make eye contact. "You ask too many questions. Stop."

He paced the floor, stopping to stare out a window that looked out on the ski hill. He checked his phone.

She stared down at the clusters of people. Her heart leaped when she saw Jason. He was turning in a half circle, searching the crowd.

Look this way.

A moment later, he glanced up. She pressed her hand on the glass. Could he see her?

"Get away from there."

She stepped back. Jason was eaten up by the crowd again. There had to be agents out there too. Michael said there would be.

Again, Nick checked the window that offered a view to the outside. She walked over to where he was staring. The window looked out on the base of the ski hill. A car rolled into place in an area where there was no road or parking space. A man got out and walked toward the concert hall.

"Now we can go."

"What? I thought we were meeting the guy up here." Something felt really wrong. Why the constant changing of plans? Clearly, Nick had been waiting for the man with the car to show up.

"Don't argue with me, Isabel. This is how it works." He leaned close to her, his eyes like piercing daggers. "Are you all in or not?"

Sweat trickled down the back of her neck. She struggled to keep the tone of her voice even. "Course I am."

Something about the look in his eyes was darker and more threatening than she had ever seen before with him.

He led her back down the stairs and out to where the car was parked. She hesitated in her step. "Where's the buyer?"

He yanked her along. "We'll meet him."

She planted her feet, unable to move, yet knowing that she needed to go through with this to win Nick's loyalty.

He turned to face her. "Having second thoughts?"

"This just seems a little crazy." Maybe he was testing her.

"Get in the car." He grinned at her and alarm bells went off in her head. The look on his face told her everything she needed to know.

Nick knew. He knew that she was undercover. Somehow he'd figured it out. He'd been upset after the phone call. Maybe that was it.

She turned to run, but he grabbed her and tackled her.

He sat on her stomach, held her hands down and put his face very close to hers. "Do you think I'm dumb? Is that it, Isabel?"

She shook her head. "Please... I..." What could she say? How could she get out of this?

"I was going to let you in on this. It could have been like old times." He put his face so close to hers their noses almost touched. "Traitor. No one betrays Nick Solomon and lives to tell about it."

His words were a knife in her chest.

"You are dumb," he said. "I took you through that concert hall so we could lose your tail." He got off her. "Yeah, that's what the phone call was about. One of my guys spotted the tail on me."

She flipped over, intending to get to her feet and run. But he grabbed her by the back of her collar and swung her around. "Do you see how important I am? I arranged for this car to be dropped off by the organization I work for. No one crosses me."

Her fear ramped up a notch. "I'm so sorry." The words fell flat. Nothing she could say at this point would stop the volcano from erupting.

"Get over to the car." His rage was out of control. He pulled out his gun.

"We're driving somewhere secluded. Now move."

Isabel stepped toward the car, knowing that it was just a matter of time before she was dead.

When he'd seen a car park off by itself and a man walk away from it, Jason had grown suspicious. He'd decided to circle the building after losing Isabel in the concert hall. Sure enough, the car was unlocked and the keys were in the ignition. Hiding in the back seat, he'd slipped inside to wait and observe. A moment later, Nick and Isabel came out of the back of the concert hall. He'd watched as Nick pulled a gun on Isabel. They'd struggled. Rage rose up in him, but he remained still. He couldn't hear their conversation. If he showed himself, their cover would be blown.

Isabel got into the driver's side of the car. Still pointing the gun at her, Nick slipped into the front passenger seat. Jason pressed even lower in the back seat.

"Nick, you don't want to do this." Isabel's voice vibrated with intense terror.

"Start the car."

She turned the key in the ignition and shifted into gear.

"To think that I pledged my undying love to you." Nick's voice filled with rage.

Jason tried to assess what was going on. Nick seemed especially agitated. Were they still going to meet the buyer or had something changed?

She pressed the gas pedal and eased toward the road, driving slow. "This is rough going. It'll take a minute to get to the road."

"Quit making excuses, Isabel." Nick's voice dripped with sarcasm when he said Isabel's name. "You're going to die. No one betrays me."

So their cover was blown. Jason leaped up from behind the seat and reached to get the gun from Nick.

"Jump out."

While the car was still rolling, Isabel pushed the door open. She disappeared. He prayed she'd been able to roll clear of the tires.

Nick and Jason continued to struggle. The gun went off, and Nick held on to it.

The car hit something and shuddered to a stop. Both Jason and Nick were jolted by the crash. Jason pushed the door open and crawled out. He was still wobbly on his feet from the impact. Up ahead, he saw the dark figure of Isabel lying on the ground.

Nick stepped out and leaped on Jason. The two men wrestled. Nick must have dropped the gun when the car hit the curb.

Nick got on top of Jason and landed a blow to his face that sent stinging pain all through his skull. Jason's vision blurred. He struggled to get some leverage.

"Get off him." Isabel's voice sliced through the darkness as she wrapped her arm around Nick's neck and tried to pull him off.

Nick turned on her, trying to take her to the ground. Jason scrambled to his feet, grabbed Nick, spun him around and hit him once in the face and once in the stomach. Nick doubled over.

Jason grabbed Isabel's hand, but Nick blocked their way back to the concert hall. They'd have to double back to get to where people and help were. He'd lost his cell phone in the struggle with Nick.

They took off running. Nick sprinted back toward the car, probably to look for the gun.

They ran up the empty ski hill.

A gunshot sounded behind them, spurring them to run faster. Another gunshot, even closer. The ski hill was frozen and slick. Nick was gaining on them.

They neared the chairlift. Jason flipped the

switch to turn it on. The lift eased to life as he and Isabel got on.

Jason looked over his shoulder. Nick had gotten on four or five chairs behind them. Far enough away that it would not be an easy shot to make with a pistol.

Jason wiggled in his chair, then lifted and dropped his legs like he was on a swing.

"What are you doing?"

"A moving target is harder to hit."

Several more shots were fired. One pinged off the metal of the chair.

"We're going to have to jump before we get to the exit platform." He stared down. The lift had elevated them a good thirty feet above the ground. He could wait until the distance was closer to ten or fifteen feet. The snow down at the base of the hill had been hard packed and icy. Maybe they could hope for some powder and a softer landing toward the top of the mountain.

"Now?" said Isabel.

She pointed at the landing platform up ahead.

Jason glanced over his shoulder. He could make out the outline of Nick's body four seats behind them. "Let's do this."

He flipped around, slipped off the chair and hung on to it before letting go. He sailed through the air. His knees buckled from his collision with the ground, and he rolled a few feet. Isabel still hung from the chair. She let go and fell to the ground below. Hearing her moan as she landed, he prayed nothing had been broken.

The concert hall was just a set of distant glowing lights barely discernible through the trees clustered on the mountain. Nick had dropped from the lift, as well.

Jason sprinted over to Isabel and grabbed her hand to help her to her feet. "You all right?"

"Just a little shaky."

Nick was setting an intense pace as he ran toward them.

This was a remote black-diamond part of the ski hill.

Jason led Isabel toward the shelter of the trees. The canopy blocked much of the snowfall from gathering on the forest floor, allowing them to move faster and not leave many tracks.

They ran until they were both out of breath. The forest thinned, and they were out in the open again. A light winked on and off as if moving over hills, appearing and disappearing.

"Snowmobile," said Jason. "Maybe ski patrol."

"Or Nick called in reinforcements. He was able to arrange for that car to be dropped off." Isabel came up beside him.

She might be right. The snowmobile rounded

another hill. He heard the hum of a motor as it drew closer. Maybe they should hide until they were sure the snowmobiler was one of the good guys.

He couldn't see Nick anywhere.

As Isabel pointed toward a sign that showed a map of the trails on the mountains, the headlight of the snowmobile pointed directly at them.

They hurried over to the sign and crouched behind it. The snowmobile worked its way up and down the mountain. Jason peered around the sign. It was too dark to see anything but the outline of the snowmobile and its rider.

The snowmobile was set to idle. A shadowy figure emerged from the tree on the other side of the black-diamond run. The figure walked toward the idling snowmobiler, shouted above the hum of engine and then got on the back behind the driver. The voice had been loud enough so they could tell that it was Nick. He had called in reinforcements.

The snowmobile worked its way back up the mountain.

Now was their chance to run. Without a word, they both took off.

The snowmobiler stopped at the top of the trail run on a ledge. A moment later, a powerful searchlight illuminated sections of the mountain piece by piece.

Jason led Isabel toward an overhang of snow that was used for jumps. They hid underneath it, the shadows covering them as the searchlight swept past.

After the last time they were forced to brave the cold for survival, he'd prayed it wouldn't happen again. But here they were, Isabel pressed close to him, shivering. Though she was dressed for winter, they had been out in the elements for at least half an hour.

He wrapped an arm around her and whispered in her ear. "It won't be long now. They'll give up."

They'd be warmer if they could stay on the move. The hum of the snowmobile still pressed on his ears. They couldn't run…not yet.

He drew Isabel even closer.

Ten minutes passed before the snowmobile noise faded.

"Let's get back over to the chairlift."

"What if they are waiting there for us?"

They could both get hypothermia by the time they made it down the mountain on foot.

The wind blew, chilling his skin. Isabel wrapped her arms around her body. He'd skied these hills all through high school. "There are warming huts around here. At least there used to be." That would give them time to come up with a plan.

He ran down the hill back toward the map.

Isabel stood beside him as he leaned close to the map to see better. "There used to be a warming hut by the Crystal run. If memory serves."

"I'll take your word for it. I never skied."

He started walking in the general direction he thought the hut might be. "Really? I thought everyone in Silver Strike skied. I lived fifty miles up the road and made it almost every weekend."

She hurried to keep up with him as they cut across the ski run. "Mom said it was a rich person's sport." A note of sadness filled her voice.

There were all sorts of programs for kids who couldn't afford to ski to get help. His father had signed him up for everything he could. Isabel's mother just hadn't wanted to make the effort. "Maybe I'll have to take you sometime."

"Once it's okay for us to go back out in the open, right?"

Both of them had targets on their backs. Now that the smugglers knew they were being watched, the whole investigation was tainted. "Maybe we should just focus on getting down the mountain."

"I appreciate the offer." He detected warmth in her voice.

They trudged ahead. He tuned in to his surroundings, listening for the sound of the snowmobile.

The warming hut was right where he remembered it. They slipped inside out of the wind. It had benches on three sides and a fire pit in the center that was usually lit on cold days when the ski hill was operating. They sat down on one of the benches.

"If we could just build a small fire." Isabel sounded like her teeth were chattering.

"We'd be spotted, Isabel."

He took his down coat off. She was wearing a wool dress coat. "Here, come closer. We can wrap up in this, use our body heat to get warm."

She slipped out of her wool coat, wrapped her arms around his waist and pressed close to him while he formed an insulating shell with the two coats.

"Better?"

She nodded. "I'm only doing this because I'm freezing."

"Oh, come on. You like me a little bit." He hoped she picked up on his joking tone.

"I like you more than a little bit."

"Really?" She had given a forthright response to his half-joking comment. He felt like he was glowing all over. Isabel liked him.

"It's just that after Nick, I decided maybe dating wasn't my thing. Something inside me died after him. I don't know how to explain it."

"Yeah, I watched my dad get burned real bad by my mom. He never dated after that."

Watching his father in so much pain had made him conclude that maybe love was not all it was chalked up to be. The little bit he'd dated had only confirmed that. It seemed he attracted women who only knew how to take and to hurt.

He drew her closer until she stopped shivering. Even if there couldn't be anything between them and despite these trying circumstances, there was something really wonderful about holding Isabel.

"You warmed up?"

She nodded. "Maybe we should try to get to that chairlift. It would be faster."

Riskier too. Since Nick and his friend weren't chasing them down, they were probably watching the lift. "I don't know. Once that lift started to move, it would be like a red flag if they're anywhere close by."

"Jason, I know I was against it before, but I don't know if I can make it hiking down." She held up her hands covered by the leather gloves. "I can't feel my fingertips."

He weighed their options. It would take twice as long to walk down and that was if they weren't chased. They'd have to move from one cluster of trees to another, and even then they'd be out in the open some of the time.

"Let's get over to the lift. We can figure out if it's being watched." They both rose to their feet, facing each other. He reached out and squeezed her hands. "Try to keep your hands in your pockets."

She nodded. "I really messed up. Nick had his suspicions about me from the start. Otherwise, why would he have asked someone to figure out if he was being tailed?"

He pulled his glove off and touched her cold cheek. "Don't blame yourself. The Bureau could have been more careful about their tails."

"The investigation is going to fall apart because of me." Her voice faltered. "And Nick won't go to prison."

He gathered her into his arms, holding her close. "We don't know what is going to happen."

The best-case scenario was that the FBI would have to lie low with the investigation and hope the smuggling would resume once the thieves thought the heat was off. They'd been so close too, one person away from identifying the mastermind behind the whole thing.

He drew Isabel even closer. All he could think about right now was comforting Isabel and giving her some hope.

He spoke into her ear. "We'll get off this mountain and we'll get it figured out."

"We. I like the sound of that." She stepped back, swiped at her eyes and tilted her head. "Thank you, Jason."

"No problem." He pressed his hand against her

cheek, wishing they could stay in the warmth of this moment forever...but that wasn't possible.

The wind gusted and swirled around them when they stepped outside. They ran in the general direction of the chairlift, using the trees for cover and shelter whenever possible.

The silhouette of the chairlift came into view. They crouched low by the trees. A moment later, the lights of the snowmobile appeared at the top of the hill and traveled in a circle. The motor hummed as it whizzed past them. They pressed back even deeper into the trees.

Once the snowmobile was some distance from them and headed back up on the other side of the lift, Isabel spoke up. "I guess that's it, then. We go on foot." He detected the fear in her voice.

"Let's do this."

They sprinted around the trees and wove through the forest until there were no more trees to hide them. Jason glanced up the hill where he could see the headlights of the snowmobile. He and Isabel were some distance from the top of the run, but it would be just a matter of minutes before they'd be spotted. They were dark figures on a field of white—easy targets.

He prayed they had enough distance between them to get to the next cluster of trees before they were caught and killed.

FOURTEEN

Isabel's heart pounded. She willed her feet to pump faster. The buzz of the snowmobile grew louder as her boots pressed down the crunchy snow. They came to a steep part of the run.

Jason plopped onto his behind. She stared down at the incline below, which dropped off at a steep angle. It would be easier to slide than walk. She sat down beside him and pushed off with her hands.

The snowmobile would have to loop around the steep terrain. Still, the sound of its engine seemed to surround them, persistent in its pursuit.

They slid, gaining speed. She held her hands out to slow down. The searchlight swept over them as the incline leveled off. They burst to their feet and ran until they came to another steep drop-off. She slid, trying to brake with her hands. As she felt herself propelled head-first, she tucked, falling forward into a half somersault. She stopped, landing on her behind but disoriented.

Jason appeared beside her. He grabbed her arm to help her to her feet and pointed up the hill. "He's doing this the hard way."

The snowmobile, with only one rider on it, was about to make the first jump. The rider revved the motor and sailed through the air.

Both of them sprinted, half sliding and half running on the treacherous terrain. The noise of the snowmobile told her he was making the jumps and getting closer. The machine sounded like a groaning angry monster.

Then the noise stopped.

As they ran, Isabel glanced over her shoulder. The snowmobile was on its side. The rider had gotten to his feet and was lifting off his helmet, probably preparing to pursue them on foot.

Isabel dug her heels in to keep from sliding. Jason sprinted six or so feet ahead of her. She watched the back of his head in the moonlight. The reflective material on his jacket made him look like a bouncing set of stripes moving down the mountain.

The rhythm of her own rapid footsteps surrounded her. She filled her lungs with air and pumped her legs even faster, drawing close to the tree line. Her feet slid out from underneath her and she fell.

A set of hands yanked at her from the side. Before she could scream, a hand went over her mouth and she was dragged sideways. She watched the stripes of Jason's jacket disappear over a hill as Nick swung her around. He dragged her toward a cluster of evergreens. His hand slipped from her mouth.

She called Jason's name, her voice barely above a whisper and filled with desperation.

"Oh sure, call for your boyfriend." Nick loomed toward her, pulling off his gloves.

"I lost my gun somewhere." He flexed his hands. "Guess I have to do this the old-fashioned way." His words dripped with menace and an intense rage she had never seen from him before.

The blood froze in her veins.

In the distance, the sputter of a coughing engine reached her ears. The snowmobiler must have decided to try to get the machine unstuck.

She crab-walked backward to get away from Nick, knowing that nothing she could say would change his mind. He meant to kill her.

She flipped over and scrambled on all fours. Nick pounced on her, grabbing her by her collar and jerking her to her feet.

He pressed his lips close to her face, his breath like lava on her ear. "Get up. Let's get deeper into the trees so lover boy can't find us."

She tried to twist free of his grasp, which only seemed to feed his rage. Once they were hidden by trees, he swung her around and clamped his hands on her neck. As she twisted her body and struggled for breath, she kicked him in the shin. He groaned but squeezed tighter around her neck.

Her eyes watered and white dots surrounded her field of vision. She drew her hands up to his, clawing his fingers and trying to break free. She pried his fingers off enough to speak each word delivered between gasping breaths. "You. Don't. Want. To. Go. To. Prison."

His grip loosened. "What?"

Her throat felt like it had been scraped with a utility knife. "Make it look like an accident. Like I fell off one of those steep jumps." The move would buy her time and a chance at escape.

His fingers still pressed against her windpipe. "You think I'm that dumb. You're just trying to find a way to escape."

He pressed harder. She screamed, but it seemed to fade before it was out of her mouth. By now Jason would have glanced over his shoulder and come looking for her. But he'd have no way of knowing where they'd slipped into the trees.

She managed to pull his fingers away from her throat for just a moment.

"Please, Nick. Don't do this."

"Beg all you want." His hands gripped her neck even tighter, shutting off all the air.

She scratched at his fingers and tried to turn her body to break free. Her vision became a single dot of light as all the breath left her lungs. Her knees buckled. Nick pushed her so she fell on her back. She took in one sharp breath before his hands were on her neck again.

Darkness surrounded her. Her last thought was that the snow felt cold on the back of her head.

As he sprinted back up the hill, Jason mentally kicked himself. It had only been a matter of a minute that he'd run without checking over his shoulder for Isabel. Nick must have been stalking them as they moved down the hill. Jason rounded the hill. The snowmobiler had righted his machine and was revving the motor, preparing for takeoff.

Jason darted into trees to avoid being spotted. He ran. Did he dare call Isabel's name? He zigzagged around trees, pushing past the rising panic. The snowmobiler whizzed by along the tree line, his engine sputtering and humming. The headlights reached some feet into the forest. Jason ran deeper into the trees, seeing nothing. He was out of options. He'd do anything to find her.

"Isabel." He spoke her name rather than shouted it.

To the side, a rustling of tree branches caught his attention. He darted in the direction the noises had come from. Weight landed on him. He fell on his back. A fist landed a hard blow to his head while something pressed on his chest.

"She's gone, lover boy. If I can't have her, nobody can."

The thought of anything bad happening to Isabel ignited a fire inside Jason. He slammed Nick's back with his knee. The blow was enough to surprise Nick and knock him off balance. Jason landed another blow to Nick's stomach. Nick groaned and doubled over. Jason pushed him off, jumped to his feet and kicked Nick in the head just before Nick tried to pull Jason's feet out from under him. Jason hit Nick with leg jabs, one to his side and one to his head. Nick fell over and remained motionless. When Jason checked for a pulse, Nick was still alive but unconscious. Though Nick would probably only be out for a few minutes, Jason had no time or rope to restrain Nick with. His priority was finding Isabel.

Some strange energy flowed through Jason.

He refused to believe Isabel was dead. Nick must have been bluffing to weaken Jason's resolve. He ran in the direction Nick had come from, pushing tree branches out of the way. His heart beat intensely as he searched the ground made darker by the tree canopy.

He said her name not once but three times.

The snowmobile continued to patrol the perimeter of the cluster of trees. Light flashed through the trees and Jason spotted something of a light color, maybe yellow, lying on the ground. It was the knit scarf Isabel had worn with her wool dress coat.

She could have lost it in a struggle. He picked it up, held it close, picking up the scent of her floral perfume. Racing deeper into the trees, he spotted her dark form in a clearing. The porcelain skin of her face the only discernible part of her.

He dived to the ground and touched her cold cheek. Fear flooded through him at the thought of losing her. He cared deeply for her.

"Isabel."

His finger trailed down to her neck, where he felt a pulse. She was alive.

He patted her cheeks.

"I'm here." Her voice was scratchy, hoarse-sounding.

"Hey." He cradled her head.

"I must have passed out."

Nick probably heard Jason calling her name and decided to get rid of Jason before he had the chance to check to see if Isabel was still breathing.

"We don't have much time. Can you stand?"

"I think so."

He held out a hand for her and helped her up. He handed her the scarf, which she wrapped around her neck. The snowmobiler was still patrolling the tree line and Nick would be hounding them in minutes. They had no choice but to head down the mountain.

"Jason, I'm really cold." Her voice was weak. It was clear from the inflection of her words that she was giving up.

Lying on the frozen ground for at least five minutes had only brought her that much closer to hypothermia.

"We're halfway down the mountain already. If you stay with me there is a hot bath and a steaming cup of tea waiting for you at the end." He pressed his hands on either side of her cheeks. "Can you do that for me, Isabel?"

"I'm sorry I messed up the investigation. But I can't keep running like this." Her voice cracked.

He gathered her into his arms. "I know.

They'll put you in protective custody. Don't give up."

Protective custody for her seemed like the only option now. Whoever was behind all this was clearly powerful, connected and relentless.

Jason held Isabel close. Her hat felt soft against his chin.

"Let's go." Her words seemed to be undergirded with new strength. "We don't have much time."

"That's my strong lady." He kissed her on the forehead. Their eyes met momentarily. He touched her lips with his gloved hand, feeling a magnetic pull toward her as an intense warmth washed through him. He wanted to kiss her on the mouth.

He pulled back. "This time I won't lose you," he said. "Not even for a second."

As they ran through the trees, he could hear the snowmobile growing closer and then farther away as it searched for them. They moved out into the open, sliding down the steep parts of the hill.

A lamp outside the dark ski lodge came into view, a tiny light in the distance. He breathed a sigh of relief when he saw the first sign of civilization. Glancing over his shoulder at where they had emerged from the forest, he could discern moving shadows among the trees. It could be Nick.

They made their way toward the ski lodge. There would be a phone there. He quickened his pace, making sure that Isabel stayed with him.

They neared the lodge. When he'd skied here, he and his buddies had found a window with a loose latch. Maybe it hadn't been repaired even after all these years. He glanced up the hill at the sound of a motor. The snowmobile was headed their way, close enough that the men could see he and Isabel standing outside the lodge. He led Isabel around to the far side of the lodge.

The window latch was still loose. They crawled into what was the boys' locker room.

"There's probably a phone in the office," he said, taking her hand and leading her upstairs.

The door to the ski-lodge office was locked. His hope deflated. They had only minutes before the snowmobiler would be outside.

"Now what?" Her words were saturated with fear.

His mind raced. "Lost and found. People might leave cell phones."

He located the lost-and-found bins by the cafeteria just where they had been ten years ago when he'd skied here as a teen. There were bins filled with hats, orphan gloves, scarves and ski goggles and one bin filled with electronics. The first cell phone he tried was dead.

"Here, this one still has some battery left." Isabel handed it to him.

The bright lights of the snowmobile shone through the window. Both of them ducked down as he pressed in the numbers for his contact.

While he dialed, Isabel scurried across the floor and peered through the window. The main door shook. It would take Nick and his accomplice a few minutes to break in.

"Two of them got off the snowmobile and are at the door." Isabel's voice was flat, devoid of emotion. "We have to hide."

Jason held the phone to his ear. One ring. Two rings. *Come on, Michael—pick up.* The agents had to be out looking for them and waiting for a call.

Glass shattered. The men were breaking in.

Jason hurried to the far end of the cafeteria back into the boys' locker room with the phone still pressed against his ear.

Finally, Michael picked up. "Yes, who is this?"

"Help us."

"Jason, where are you?"

"We're at the ski lodge and on the run."

"I'll get a man to you as soon as I can."

"We'll be headed toward the concert venue." He doubted the concert was still going on, but maybe there would be a cleanup crew or someone still around.

The footsteps of Nick and his accomplice seemed to echo through the empty building, growing ever closer. He set the phone down. Isabel was already crawling through the window when Nick appeared in the doorway.

She glanced at Nick and then at Jason.

"Go," said Jason. "I'll catch up with you."

Nick dived for Jason. Jason hit him hard twice against the jaw. The blow caused Nick to take a step back.

Jason jumped up to the open window. Nick charged toward him again, and Jason flipped around, kicking him hard enough to make him stumble backward and fall.

The move gave Jason enough time to get out of the window. He sprinted downhill, praying that Isabel had not been captured by Nick's accomplice.

FIFTEEN

Isabel ran in the direction she thought the concert venue might be. Much of the forest in Silver Strike had been preserved, even in town, so she darted from one clump of trees to the next looking for the building. She found a snow-packed road that led downward. Sooner or later she'd run into something, but being on the road made her too easy a target. She couldn't stay on it for long.

She wondered too if Jason had made it out. Her heart ached to know that he was safe. She should have stayed behind to help him. That was what he would have done for her.

The hum of a snowmobile engine told her she needed to get off the road. She veered back into the trees. The snowmobile putted past her, clearly searching. She tore off the yellow scarf and threw it on the ground, knowing that it would make her more visible through the trees. Why hadn't she thought of that ages ago? She darted from one tree to the next, taking the time to catch her breath and peer around the trunk of a tree. As the snowmobile eased by her, she saw only one rider.

A hand squeezed her shoulder and she nearly jumped out of her skin. She swung around, ready to fight. Jason stood only inches from her. He placed a finger up to his lips, indicating to be quiet. The snowmobile faded in the distance. She looked up into Jason's eyes, blue even in the shadows of nighttime. The memory of him kissing her forehead and then touching her lips rose to the surface. His eyes had grown wide as he leaned close. She had thought he would kiss her. In that moment, she realized she wanted to feel his lips on hers. He brought to life feelings that she had long thought were dead.

He tilted his head and raised his eyebrows up toward the lodge. A gesture that indicated Nick was in the forest searching for them.

As the noise of the snowmobile died out altogether, she heard faint sounds, the crackle of a branch, a padding noise that could be footfalls on snow.

Jason wrapped his arm around her waist and eased her around to the other side of the tree. His lips brushed her forehead as they faced each other. The rhythm of his breathing surrounded her. Nick's footsteps became more distinct and louder.

The seconds ticked by. The sounds stopped as though Nick were looking around.

Her breath caught in her throat.

Judging from the volume of the footsteps, Nick was maybe ten feet away from them.

She tilted her head and looked into Jason's eyes, drawing strength from his proximity and the calm of his expression.

The footsteps resumed, this time making almost a squeaking sound on crunchy dry snow.

It seemed to take forever for the footsteps to get far away. Finally, the quiet of the night forest fell around them like a soft blanket.

Jason and Isabel stood very close together. Moonlight sneaked through the trees and washed over them. He bent his head and brushed his cheek over hers. Fire ignited, covering her skin and traveling through her muscles as his lips found hers. He brushed lightly over her mouth and then deepened the kiss as his hand touched her cheek.

She remained suspended in the moment, relishing a sensation like warm honey being poured over her head and dripping down her skin. He held her close for a second longer before whispering in her ear. "We're almost home free, Isabel."

The kiss had made her dizzy, light-headed. "Yes, I suppose we should make a run for it."

He kissed her one more time, took her hand and led her through the thick of the trees until they were able to run. There were no lights on at the concert venue, but the silhouette of the huge building was plain enough. There were only two snow-covered cars in the parking lot as they approached. Snowmobile tracks indicated the other pursuer had circled the building at least twice.

She looked over her shoulder. Nick emerged from the trees, running straight for them. The snowmobile came around the side of the building.

Jason pivoted and she followed. An SUV turned off the road into the lot. Michael's car.

The snowmobile made a beeline for them, the clanging of the motor pressing on her ears as she sprinted toward Michael's car. Jason got there first, swinging open the back door. She piled in and Jason got in behind her.

Michael revved the motor and sped forward, swerving and fishtailing through the icy lot. The snowmobile blocked their exit. Michael hit the accelerator and drove over a snow-covered lawn back up to the road.

The snowmobile followed them until they turned onto a plowed road. Nick stood at the edge of the parking lot. The stiffness of his posture suggested rage.

"Good timing, Michael," said Jason.

"We aim to please," said Michael. "We've got a temporary safe house set up for you. You'll both need to be debriefed, but I imagine you'd like to get a good night's sleep first."

"I'm looking forward to a hot bath and a steaming cup of tea." She smiled at Jason. The softness in his expression, that look of affection in his eyes, made her heart skip a beat.

"As promised." He placed his gloved hand over hers and squeezed.

She pressed her shoulder against his, still caught up in the exhilaration of their kiss.

Jason leaned forward to talk to Michael. "So is the investigation blown?"

"We'll have to lie low for a while until they think we've backed off. Once things cool down, we've got quite a few people to keep an eye on, especially Nick Solomon, thanks to Isabel."

She was glad Michael saw it that way.

Michael said, "The profiler thinks the kingpin is working class or came from humble roots because of what Isabel told us about getting a thrill out of making the wealthy uncomfortable in their own homes."

They drove on in silence. Jason put an arm around Isabel and she rested her head against his chest, listening to his heart beat. The heaviness of fatigue invaded her body and she closed her eyes.

She was safe…for now.

Nick was still out there. Still set on her demise.

Jason rolled over on the bed as sunlight streamed through the blinds of the safe house. He'd had only a few hours' sleep before morning came. He intended to get a few more. The safe house was a three-story affair in a subdivision outside of town that had gone belly-up. They'd driven past half-finished homes, some just framed, others nearly complete. The outside walls of the house they were in were done, but he could look across the floor to where Isabel slept on a mattress inside a room that had only two-by-fours for walls. In order for this to be a functional safe house, the Bureau had gotten the plumbing in the bathroom and kitchen done. Electrical wires were exposed in the kitchen where the drywall had not been put up before the stove and refrigerator were put in place.

Isabel had had to settle for a hot shower instead of a bath, but he had been able to give her a steaming cup of tea.

Only one agent, playing solitaire at the kitchen

table, watched over them, his gun belt slung over a chair.

Jason tossed and turned several times before he realized it was an act of futility to try to sleep. He sat up on his bed.

Isabel looked peaceful covered in a soft pink blanket drawn up over her shoulders. Her cheeks had a rosy glow. The kiss they'd shared had been wonderful, but it had probably been brought on by the terror they were in the midst of at the time. He doubted the attraction would survive once this was all over, if it was ever over. He intended to return to his work as a PI even if the Bureau didn't need him anymore. He could take care of himself. But Isabel might need to go into witness protection as long as Nick Solomon was at large. She'd have to move and change her name, cut all her connections. No, as much as he cared for her, he couldn't see a future with her where she would be safe unless they caught Nick.

Jason rose to his feet and ambled into the kitchen. He was still dressed in his clothes from the night before. The agent gave him a nod. He swung the refrigerator door open. It was fully stocked.

"I'm going to get some air," said the agent. He rose to his feet, shrugged into his ski jacket and stepped out the back door.

The subdivision was miles from town, surrounded by forest. Jason didn't relish the confinement. Hopefully, he'd be back to work in a day or so. First, he needed to make sure the Bureau took care of Isabel.

Jason broke some eggs into a bowl and stirred them with a fork. The bacon sizzled when he placed it on the griddle. He melted butter in a frying pan and poured the egg mixture in.

The aroma of bacon filled the air.

"One of my favorite smells in the world." In her room, Isabel sat up on her mattress. She gathered the blanket around her and strode into the kitchen.

"I made enough for two. I don't think the agent is hungry. Saw some orange juice in the fridge if you want to pour some."

She retrieved some glasses and the juice and then settled on one of the stools at the island where Jason was cooking. Bruises on her neck from where Nick had tried to strangle her were still visible. The thought of that man touching her enraged him. He served up their food and pushed the plate toward her.

Isabel made sounds of approval as she ate. She looked up at him with her doe eyes, and he was struck by how beautiful she was. Affection glowed on her face. "My compliments to the chef."

He could pretend this was some sort of scene of domestic bliss, even imagine that they might have something like this waiting in their future. But he had to be realistic. They both did.

"How long are they going to make us stay in this house? I want to get back to work and I need to call my boss."

"Isabel, I don't know if you can just go back to that."

Her forehead creased. "I want my life back, Jason."

"Whoever is behind this has a lot of power and isn't opposed to violent solutions," Jason said. "You've seen that for yourself."

Her mouth formed a flat line as she pressed her lips together. "But this will end soon, won't it?"

"Not while Nick is still out there. Be realistic. You might need to think about witness protection."

"I'm not giving up the life I've built here." She stared at the ceiling for a moment. "Can't you stay with me until they catch him?"

"I don't know," Jason said. "I think you need more protection than I can provide." Guilt washed through him. If he had been paying attention, Nick wouldn't have been able to strangle Isabel.

Her eyes became glassy with tears. "What are you saying?"

"I'm saying I don't want you to die. I'm saying the best thing is for you to move to another town with a new name."

She shook her head. "I thought... I don't know. That something was happening between us."

He took her empty plate. More than anything, he wanted to hold her. To tell her everything would be okay and that they could be together, but that might get her killed. He made his voice sound cold and distant on purpose. "I'm only thinking of your safety."

"My safety?" A single tear rolled down her cheek. "I need to go brush my teeth." She jumped off the stool and disappeared around the corner. The bathroom at least was Sheetrocked and had a door.

Jason put the plates in the sink and stared out the window. There were boot tracks outside, but he didn't see the agent anywhere.

He could hear Isabel running the water in the bathroom.

Feeling uneasy, he put on his boots and slipped into his coat. He stepped outside onto the threshold, visually following the tracks that went some distance from the house. He took a few more steps away from the house. The footprints ended and were replaced by drag marks leading to another half-finished house.

Heart racing, he turned and sprinted back into the house. The agent could take care of himself. It was Isabel he was worried about.

Isabel splashed water on her face and stared at herself in the bathroom mirror. She pulled a strand of blond hair behind her ear. So that was it. She'd opened her heart to Jason, let herself feel something for him and he was pushing her away.

Of course, it wasn't realistic that they go into witness protection together. They'd known each other less than a week, but he acted like he didn't want to be with her at all. He'd kept her safe so far. Maybe he was just looking for an excuse to push her away. He could be scared of his feelings for her or he might have just been caught up in the moment when he kissed her. It didn't matter. The point was she wasn't going to open herself up to this kind of stinging pain. Not ever again.

She reached for a towel. The back door opened. Jason must have been coming back inside. She'd heard him step out earlier.

She patted her face dry, covering her eyes. Footsteps echoed down the hallway.

She wasn't about to call out to Jason. The last thing she wanted to do was talk to him.

She replaced the towel on the bar, then realized she hadn't heard the back door close. The bathroom door swung open. Before she could turn, a gun pressed into the middle of her back.

"Thought you'd get away from me, huh? You scream, I'll shoot." Nick wrapped his arm around her waist and pointed the gun at her head. "Lover boy is distracted right now. Don't expect him to come rescue you."

He pulled her through the door. Nick had her in such a tight hold, she couldn't move.

He half lifted, half dragged her through the snow into one of the other incomplete houses. He pushed her onto the plywood floor and pulled a bandanna out of his pocket. Diving to the floor, he grabbed hold of her hair. "Hold still."

Her head stung where he'd yanked on her ponytail.

In the distance, she heard Jason call her name. He sounded so very far away.

Nick must have heard the cry, as well. Panic filled his words. He pointed the gun at her. "Cry out and you're dead." The tone of his voice told her he wasn't lying. "Give me your hands."

She flipped over and tried to crawl away,

knowing he would overpower her, but at least it bought her some time.

Jason and the agent would most likely go through the front door of the safe house and search there first. In the minutes it took them to find the tracks and drag marks at the back of the house, Nick would be able to escape with her if he had a vehicle nearby.

Nick pounced on her again, flipping her around and tying the bandanna around her wrists. He pulled her to her feet and pushed her through the empty house, their footsteps echoing on the plywood subfloor. He pushed her out the back of the house.

She heard the sound of a diesel truck before she saw it. Nick had left it running for a quick escape. He led her around to the side of the house and shoved her in the driver's seat. "Scoot over." And then he jumped behind the wheel.

The truck eased through the deep snow.

Isabel lifted her head to look out the back window. The truck bed was covered with a tarp.

"Stay down," Nick barked.

She reached for the door handle, seeking to escape before the truck was going too fast. Though her hands were bound, she was able to wrap fingers around the door handle. Nick grabbed the collar of her robe and pulled her back.

"Don't even." He pulled a gun from his waist

and pointed it at her. "Just in case you want to try that again." Nick pressed the accelerator, trying to go faster, which only made the wheels of the truck spin. He cursed.

The truck gained some traction and he sped toward the road.

The Bureau had taken great pains to make sure they weren't followed to the safe house. "How did you find me?"

"You pay someone enough money and they will tell you anything."

So one of the agents had turned on them. The investigation was even more tainted.

"Everyone has a price, Blondie." Nick sped up a winding country road. "Once we figured out the Feds were following us, it just took a little research to figure out who would turn because of debt and a gambling problem."

"Which agent?"

Nick shook his head. "I'm not telling you." He grinned. "After I deal with you, it won't take much to get rid of lover boy too."

Ice replaced the blood in her veins. Nick was going to kill Jason, as well, and she had no way to warn him that one of the agents was dirty. "Where are you taking me?"

"Someplace where they won't find you until spring, if ever. And it will look like an accident. Just like you suggested on the ski hill."

Nick stared at the road ahead as a sinister smile spread across his face. "Got to hand it to you, Blondie—you have some good ideas. We could have been such a great team. Living large." He turned to look at her as the road straightened out and his eyes were as cold as stone. "Now you won't live at all."

Terror crushed her lungs, making it hard to take in even a shallow breath.

SIXTEEN

Jason wrapped his arms around himself and drew his knees up to his chest. Even with his ski jacket on, it was chilly underneath the tarp of Nick's truck, where he'd hidden.

The truck had been rolling away as he'd jumped in the back, too fast for him to get to the cab and pull Isabel free. If the passenger-side door was locked, he would have lost his chance altogether. Nick had been distracted by Isabel trying to escape when Jason climbed in the back.

The bed of the truck vibrated as it rumbled up a hill and slipped into a curve. Once Nick stopped, Jason would have a chance to get to Isabel. It had been at least twenty minutes and Nick hadn't even slowed down.

Jason eased toward the side of the truck and peeked out at the winter landscape. Nick must be taking Isabel deep into the hills far from witnesses. He checked his pocket. Though he'd been issued another phone, he'd left it on the kitchen counter of the safe house.

He rolled back to the middle of the truck bed. His hand wrapped around a tire iron. That might come in handy.

He focused on the rhythm of the wheels turning for what must have been another twenty minutes.

Finally, the truck lurched to a stop. He heard the driver's-side door open and slam shut. Then the passenger door eased open. He waited for at least three minutes before lifting the tarp and peering above the rim of the truck bed.

He didn't see Nick or Isabel, but their tracks were easy enough to follow. They'd gone toward a cluster of trees. He grabbed the tire iron and jumped to the ground, pressing close to the truck to avoid being seen if they came back out.

He ran toward the forest, then dashed from tree to tree. Nick shouted something at Isabel, disturbing the quiet forest. Fearing for her life, Jason sprinted through the evergreens. An old log cabin leaning to one side stood in a clearing. Nick stomped past a glassless window. Jason lifted his head but couldn't see Isabel anywhere.

Jason edged closer as fear was embedded in every muscle of his body. What if he was too late? He dashed toward another tree and then crouched as he approached the house. At least he hadn't heard a gunshot.

Nick's voice rose above the sound of scuffling. "If they ever find you, it will look like you froze to death. My hands will be clean. We are miles from everything. No one comes up this road this time of year."

Jason raised his head above the rim of the window. Isabel lay on the floor with Nick kneeling beside her, removing the bandanna that bound her hands.

Isabel was still in pajamas and a robe. Her feet must be icicles by now in the slippers she wore.

His tire iron was no match for the gun he saw in Nick's waistband. Because he'd just gotten up less than an hour ago, he hadn't had time to grab his own gun.

If he could surprise Nick, Jason might be able to overtake him. Nick stepped through the door on the opposite wall from where Jason was hidden.

Isabel rose to her feet.

Jason made a hissing noise to try to get her attention. She saw him just as Nick, standing in the doorway, turned in the direction of the sound. Jason ducked down behind the cabin wall.

"Did you say something, Isabel?" Nick's voice dripped with suspicion.

"Sorry I made that noise. I just wish you'd reconsider what you're doing here," Isabel said.

Nick stomped back into the doorway. "No one betrays me and gets away with it. You stay in this cabin while I drive away." He lifted the gun and pointed it at her. "Don't try to follow me."

Jason pressed against the cabin wall, waiting for the sound of Nick's retreating footsteps. A long heavy silence followed. Nick halted.

"You win," said Isabel.

The answer must have satisfied Nick because he stomped away. Jason hurried around the side of the cabin. Nick was still in view with his back to the cabin. Isabel's footsteps pounded inside the cabin.

Nick spun around. Jason shrank back along the side wall, hoping he hadn't been spotted.

"I said stay in there. Go sit in a corner," Nick said. His voice filled with rage.

Nick must be able to see Isabel through the glassless windows.

Isabel's light footfall padded on the wood floor of the cabin.

Jason pressed against the wall, unable to gauge where Nick was at. The guy had almost a sixth sense for when he was under threat. Jason needed to wait, but if they waited too long, they would miss their ride out of here.

He peered out from the side of the cabin. Nick

was nowhere in sight. The trees hid the view of the truck.

He dashed to the front of the cabin and stuck his head in the door. "Hurry."

She ran toward him. He reached a hand out for her.

Through the trees, the sound of the diesel truck starting up reached them. Isabel seemed to understand the plan without his having to explain. If they couldn't get under that tarp without being spotted, they would both freeze out here.

He slipped behind a tree.

Nick would take a few minutes to let the engine warm up before taking off down the road. They'd have to jump in once the truck was rolling and Nick's focus was on his driving.

The grind of gears shifting reached Jason's ears. He ran out toward the tailgate. The truck couldn't be going faster than five miles an hour. Still, it was a challenge to climb over the tailgate quietly. He reached out a hand for Isabel, who struggled to run in her sheepskin slippers. She leaped and got a foothold on the bumper, then piled in. Glancing over his shoulder to a view of the back of Nick's head, Jason lifted the tarp and they rolled under it. He drew her close so they were completely covered.

She was shivering. He unzipped his coat,

drew her to his chest and wrapped the coat around her.

He listened to the rumbling of the truck motor. Her soft hair brushed his chin as her shivering subsided.

"Are your feet cold?"

"Some. The sheepskin lining is pretty warm," she whispered.

He prayed Nick would stop at a gas station soon. Somewhere public so they could slip out before Nick noticed the extra lumps beside his toolbox underneath the tarp.

"Jason, one of the agents is dirty. That's how Nick found the safe house."

"Really?" Not Michael, surely not Michael. Yet they couldn't take a chance until they knew for sure. They were on their own for now.

The truck continued to rumble on, though the change in pitch of the rolling tires told him the road had gone from snow packed to paved. They must be getting close to something.

The truck slowed and the road changed again. Judging from the sound the tires made, they might be on dirt. Finally, Nick braked and turned off the engine. The truck door eased open and slammed shut. Jason didn't hear any retreating footsteps.

Jason tensed, fearing they'd been spotted beneath the tarp.

Isabel gasped. She pressed closer to him.

Tension covered them like a shroud as they lay still, clinging to each other and praying.

The vague padding of footsteps in snow pressed on his ears. He remained still, not even daring to breathe yet.

When he could hear no more noise, he rolled free of Isabel, turned over and lifted the tarp just enough to see above the edge of the truck. Isabel scooted beside him to watch, as well. They were parked in what was in the summertime a recreation area with picnic tables, playground equipment and a lake. But this time of year, it was completely abandoned.

Nick had walked less than twelve feet away from the truck, too close for them to risk climbing out. The closest hiding place was a cluster of bare bushes by the lake.

Nick's back was to them. He checked something on his phone and peered toward the road as if waiting for someone. A car appeared around the curve leading into the parking lot. It stopped, and Nick walked toward it as a woman in a uniform, maybe a maid's, got out. She handed Nick an envelope.

Now was their chance, while Nick was distracted. Isabel followed as Jason crawled under the tarp to the far side of the truck away from Nick.

Jason slipped out from beneath the tarp. He

was exposed for only a second as he swung his leg over the side of the truck and crouched down. As Isabel did the same, Jason could hear the car starting up and speeding out of the snowy parking lot.

Nick got into his truck and started it up. The motor ran for several minutes warming up while both of them crouched close to the passenger side. Isabel rested her hand on Jason's back. They'd be seen if they made a run for it now.

If Nick pulled out and didn't look back, they'd have a chance.

Jason's gaze darted from the picnic table to the bushes a little farther away.

The truck eased forward. Heart racing, Jason glued his gaze to the back of Nick's head. Even the slightest movement meant they were dead.

Isabel dashed toward the picnic table. Nick's head tilted as though he were checking his rearview mirror. His truck continued to roll forward.

Jason froze. He was exposed, but movement might alarm Nick, as well. The truck reached the edge of the parking lot.

Isabel crouched on the far side of the picnic table, which didn't entirely conceal her. She was probably cold again. It wasn't that far back to the edge of town, but it would be an arduous journey for her dressed the way she was.

Nick's truck rumbled as it pulled out onto the road.

Jason raced toward the picnic table. The truck disappeared around the curve.

He reached Isabel. "There's a hiking trail on the other side of the lake. Houses at the end of it."

They sprinted through the snow. He was grateful it was only a few inches deep.

They both heard the rumble of the diesel truck at the same time.

Nick had turned around and was headed straight for them. His big truck lumbered over the barriers in the parking lot and bore down on them.

They edged toward the frozen lake, running along the bank. Nick's truck turned around. The driver's-side window rolled down.

Jason caught the glint of metal just before the first shot was fired. He stepped out onto the frozen lake. The ice looked thick and solid. Across was the fastest way to get to the trailhead and the shelter of the trees there. He knew the lake was solid. Kids played hockey on it.

Nick got out of his truck and fired several more shots.

Isabel reached for Jason's hand. The ice cracked around her where a shot was fired.

"Hurry." He could see the trailhead not more than twenty yards away. Nick fired another shot.

An eerie quiet descended around them, their feet tapping on the ice the only noise. He looked over his shoulder. Nick was headed back up the bank toward his truck. Probably to swing around to the road to try to catch them on the trailhead before they could get to a house.

They came to the edge of the lake. "We'll have to cut through the trees. He'll be waiting for us at the end of the trailhead."

The trees were more like tall bare bushes. Within minutes, the menacing sound of the diesel truck reached Jason's ears. Would Nick come in after them or just wait for them to emerge?

The brush became thick and hard to navigate through.

"We can't go back." Isabel's whisper filled with panic.

The bright colors of Jason's coat would be easy enough to see if Nick chose to come in after them.

"Get low," Jason whispered as he squeezed between two bushes. They worked their way through the labyrinth of bare branches and brush.

When he lifted his head, he saw smoke rising up through the air. Someone's woodstove.

The brush ended at the edge of a property. A

small cottage-like house with a barn beside it was a welcome sight.

Isabel let out a breath. "We made it." She rushed toward the door and knocked.

Jason stood beside her. "We'll get warmed up and I'll call a friend to come get us. I don't think we should go back to my place or yours."

She cast her gaze downward. "I'm sure Nick or whoever he works for will have people watching."

A woman of about forty opened the door. She was short and round with granny glasses. She held a coffee cup in her hand. Her expression changed from confused to fearful as her eyes grew wide. "Can I help you?"

"Please," Isabel said. "I know this looks crazy." She touched her robe. "It's a long story. We just need to get warmed up and use your phone."

"I can have a friend here to pick us up in ten minutes," Jason said, hoping to allay the woman's understandable wariness.

The woman's gaze traveled from Isabel to Jason and then back to Isabel. "Okay, come in and sit by the fire."

Jason glanced from side to side, not seeing any sign of Nick or his truck. That didn't mean they were in the clear. Nick knew they were both alive. Sooner or later he'd come for them.

* * *

Though the woman at the house had grabbed a blanket for Isabel to wrap around herself, it felt like the cold had sunk down into her bones, and she would never be warm again.

Pulling the curtains to one side, Jason watched out the window. He stepped back and paced the floor. "The man I called is not connected to the Bureau in any way. He's a family friend."

If she wasn't so exhausted from running and being cold, she might be just as agitated. She drew the blanket around her shoulders.

Despair sank even deeper into her bones than the cold, down to the marrow. She was tired, hungry and scared. They couldn't count on help from the Bureau until the turncoat was outed. She couldn't go back to her cozy apartment.

The woman brought Isabel a steaming cup of coffee. "Here you go, dear."

"Thank you so much for your kindness," Isabel said.

"We'll be out of your hair in a few minutes," Jason said. "My friend doesn't live too far from here."

The woman nodded and disappeared into the kitchen.

Jason peered out the window again. He whirled

around, swinging his hand up and down. "Get out of view."

Isabel jumped up. Her coffee splashed in the cup as she moved away from the window and stood beside Jason.

"His truck went by. Going real slow."

So Nick was trolling the neighborhood looking for them. "We can go to the police and tell them we're being stalked. They'll pick Nick up."

"That's a short-term solution. They'll hold him for a few hours and then someone from the organization will bail him out," Jason said. "I can't tell the police anything about the investigation."

She leaned close to Jason, touching his upper arm. The desperation of their situation sank in. They really were in this alone together.

Outside in the driveway, a car pulled up and flashed its lights three times.

Jason took Isabel's hand. "That's the signal. Let's go."

Isabel put her nearly full cup of coffee on a side table and yelled a hasty thank-you to the kind woman in the kitchen. They hurried outside into the overcast gray of late afternoon. This time of year it got dark around five o'clock. They had been on the run all day.

The friend turned out to be an older man, balding and broad through the shoulders. Jason got into the front seat and Isabel slipped into the back, but not before a quick glance around. She saw no other vehicles.

As the driver backed up, Jason turned sideways. "Isabel, this is Fred. He used to be a cop and a friend of my father's."

"Pleased to meet you." The formality felt odd considering the threat they were under. *There's always time for manners.* The thought was almost sarcastic.

Fred nodded.

"Can you set us up with a place to sleep and food and maybe a car after we are rested?"

Jason seemed to have come up with some kind of plan. Right now, all she could think about was food, rest and getting warmed up.

"Can do," said Fred.

Isabel glanced over her shoulder, expecting to spot the black truck. She saw only the dark road. This part of town didn't have streetlamps.

Fred took them to a tiny apartment on the second floor of an apartment building. The living room and kitchen were tidy but very impersonal. No photographs or pictures. There was a display case with antique handguns in it and a rack on the wall that held several fishing poles.

"You should be able to find something to eat." Fred kept his boots and coat on while Isabel and Jason took off theirs. "I'll run some errands. Get her some clothes. Sleep where you're comfortable. I'll wake you in a bit." He looked at Isabel. "What size do you wear?"

"Eight."

After Fred left, Isabel opened the refrigerator and several cupboards, looking for inspiration. "Guess it's my turn to cook since you did breakfast."

Their time at the safe house felt like eons ago. For a brief moment, she had caught her breath, felt safe. But she hadn't been safe, and neither was her heart. The sting of Jason's rejection still felt raw.

Jason stood beside her, staring at the contents of the cupboard. "Lots of bachelor food."

"So tomato soup it is. There's a loaf of bread here. If there's cheese in the refrigerator, we can have some grilled cheese sandwiches too."

They worked together to make the meal. Jason buttered bread and sliced cheese while she heated the grill and stirred the soup. Again, she was struck by the contradiction of what they were doing. If anyone were to observe the scene, it would be a picture of domestic bliss, just a couple working together to make a meal.

But the whole thing was a lie. They weren't safe, and they weren't going to be together when this was all over...if it was ever over.

Metal scraped against metal when she stirred

the soup. The sound set her teeth on edge. She put the spoon down on a paper towel by the stove. Maybe it wasn't the noise that bothered her but that reality that was rapidly sinking in. They were together for now only because they had to be. The Bureau couldn't protect them.

Jason flipped over the sandwiches as an uncomfortable silence settled between them.

She had to say the words that were on the tip of her tongue since their car ride over here. "So it sounds like you have a plan. You want to use one of Fred's cars for some reason."

Jason lifted the sandwiches off the grill. "Nick is in contact with the guy who set this whole thing up. We can't depend on the Bureau for help. What if we follow Nick and he leads us to the kingpin? Since someone in this field office would leak information that could cost us our lives, we can get the information to a different field office."

"If Nick was behind bars, if the mastermind was caught, then I wouldn't have to go into witness protection. I could have my life back." Would it still be a life without Jason?

Jason's blue-eyed gaze rested on her. He nodded slowly as if thinking about what she had said. "Yes, that might be the case."

His features softened and she wondered if he

was thinking about the kiss. Did it mean anything to him at all?

She found some bowls and poured the soup into them. He carried over the sandwiches on a single plate and sat down at the table opposite her.

"Do you know where Nick lives?"

"I'm not sure. He might stay with his aunt Phoebe. I know where she lives. She's the only relative who has anything to do with him."

He took a bite of sandwich. "Then we start the surveillance there."

"Do you think the Bureau is still watching Nick?"

Jason shrugged. "Michael said they would have to lie low with the investigation for a while. Plus, that's how Nick figured out we were onto him. So I would guess not."

"The agents must be looking for us, wondering about us?"

"Unless the mole told them some lie about us, that we were dead or that we were the turncoats."

Isabel dipped her spoon into the soup. The meal had always been good comfort food when she was a kid. A neighbor lady who felt sorry for her made it, but right now she could barely taste the soup.

The plan was risky. What if Nick figured out

he was being followed? Their future was filled with so much uncertainty. The potential to end up dead was huge.

She took in a breath and shifted in her chair. "I guess that's what we have to do."

Jason placed his hand over hers. "I wish it could be some other way."

His touch brought back the memory of the kiss. She pulled her hand away as a barb shot straight through her heart. Did he feel anything at all for her?

"I know it's really dangerous. I wish there was a way for you to be safe and to have your life back."

"I'm afraid. Can we pray?" Whatever happened to them, God would always be with her.

He nodded. "We should have done that a long time ago."

Jason bowed his head and she folded her hands and closed her eyes, as well.

She started. "Lord, we need Your guidance and protection. Please help us to bring Nick and this other man to justice."

After a second of silence, Jason said, "We are both really afraid. Would You show us the right course of action?"

She lifted her head and looked across the table at Jason.

"Amen," said Jason.

There seemed to be a warmth in his expression, but maybe she was seeing what she wanted to see.

"Let's get some sleep. I'll take the couch. You can have the bed."

Isabel snuggled under the comforter and was asleep within minutes. She was awakened by Jason shaking her shoulder. "Time to get up. Time to go."

He clicked on the light beside her bed. She winced, still trying to clear her brain of the fog of sleep. "How long was I out?"

"Three hours. It'll be enough to keep us going." He held up two shopping bags. "Fred got you some warm clothes. And a phone for me."

Isabel dressed quickly.

When they stepped outside, it was pitch dark. She could see her breath as she exhaled. Though her cheeks chilled from the cold, she felt snug and warm in the ski jacket Fred had gotten for her.

"The car is in the underground parking lot."

Jason led her into the dimly lit garage where the car was stored along with ten others that must belong to the people in the apartment complex.

Isabel got into the passenger seat. She breathed in one final prayer and then her gaze rested on Jason as he buckled himself in behind the wheel.

"Let's do this," she said even as the fear squeezed tight around her chest.

SEVENTEEN

"Surveillance is actually very boring," said Jason. They'd stopped for coffee at an all-night kiosk before parking outside the trailer court where Nick's aunt lived. "A lot of sitting and waiting."

Isabel took a sip of her steaming beverage and tilted her head toward the ceiling. "I just hope this works." She tugged on the collar of her shirt.

Her voice was tempered with anxiety. He didn't blame her. If there was some place he thought he could hide her where she would be safe from all this, he would have taken her there in a heartbeat.

There was only one entrance to the court and they'd spotted Nick's truck outside the trailer when they'd circled through. If Nick left, it would be easy enough to tail him.

"Sometimes the waiting can be more nerve-racking than the tailing," Jason said.

"Did you always want to be a detective?"

"I kind of fell into it. My father was in law enforcement. I made it through the academy but hated all the paperwork once they put me on the force." He took a sip of his coffee. "How about you? You can't tell me you played property manager with your dolls when you were little."

She laughed. "No, I did what every little girl did. Put a wedding dress on the doll and pretended she married the boy doll, moved into their town house with the cool plastic furniture and lived happily ever after."

"I know some people find happily-ever-after. I've seen it at church. Looking at them from the outside, anyway."

"You're a pessimist about true love?"

"It's just I saw my father torn to pieces by his belief in happily-ever-after. I saw the way a woman could destroy a good man."

"It works both ways, Jason. Men shred women too." Her words were drenched in pain.

"Sorry. I'm sure Nick was no picnic."

She shook her head. "I was very young and very naive. I thought when a man said he loved you, he didn't have ulterior motives." She turned her head and stared out the window and then glanced in his direction.

It felt as though a wall had gone up between them. Like there was something going unsaid.

The kiss had meant so much to him, but he wouldn't risk her life so they could be together. He didn't want to send her any more mixed messages.

She took another sip of coffee. "I had this big hole in my heart because of my childhood that really only God could fill. But when I was a teenager, I thought having a boyfriend would make it better."

"You've overcome so much, Isabel." He couldn't help but admire the woman sitting beside him. The only thing that meant more to him than the kiss was their prayer together.

A soft smile graced her face. Then she turned to watch through the windshield. "I've been thinking. That woman who met Nick at the recreation area. I recognize the uniform shirt she wore. It's for Happy Homes, a maid service. Sun and Ski uses them for cleaning jobs sometimes."

"Interesting. What do you suppose she was giving him?" Jason said.

"Well, I don't think it was a sentimental card or a grocery list. They were meeting in an out-of-the-way place." Isabel continued to stare straight ahead.

"It would have to be something you couldn't send in a text or you didn't want a record of. Maybe cash or instructions," he said. Something about the clandestine meeting place suggested the maid might be connected to Nick's illegal activities.

They'd been sitting and waiting for over an hour. What if this didn't work? They could hide out at Fred's for a few days. But Jason didn't want to put his friend at risk after he'd been so kind.

Isabel sat up a little straighter. "Headlights."

He leaned to see better through the glass. The lights were high enough to be a truck. It had to be close to midnight. Whoever was leaving at this time was up to no good.

They were parked off to the side of the trailer-court entrance behind the sign that gave its name. Their headlights were off.

The truck rumbled by without stopping.

"It's him, all right." Jason placed his fingers on the key but didn't turn it.

Nick's taillights were still visible. The turn signal on the truck blinked. Jason started the car and turned onto the road.

With little to no traffic, and as hypervigilant as Nick was, tailing was going to be tricky.

Jason rolled down the road and turned where Nick had turned. Nick was headed back toward town. That was good. A greater possibility of other cars. Late-night revelers on their way home.

Jason stayed back, grateful that the road into town was straight. One other car got between them before they entered the city limits. Once in town, he was able to take some side streets and still track Nick. The truck stayed on the main street of Silver Strike, went all the way through town and then exited on the other side. They passed a car dealership with dark windows and drove a little way out to the country.

Jason pulled off the road onto a shoulder.

"What are you doing? We'll lose him."

"We're the only car out here. I don't want him to get suspicious. There are only three or four places he could turn off out this way. Some businesses, a few homes, I think."

They waited in silence. The snowfall had intensified since they'd left the trailer park. After a few minutes, Jason pulled back out onto the road. They passed a home set back from the road. No black truck was parked by it. They drove by a meat-processing business where no cars were parked.

Isabel wiggled in her seat. "What if we lost him?"

"We'll go a little farther." Jason checked his rearview mirror. His real fear was that Nick was onto them and had pulled off the road, waiting to come up behind them.

Isabel lifted off her seat a little and pointed. "There."

Up the hill was a large warehouse-looking

building teeming with activity. Nick's truck was parked outside, as were several others illuminated by the outdoor lamps. Light glowed in the windows of the building.

Jason turned off the main road. There was a car in front of him headed in the same direction as well as one behind him. Something was going on.

He pulled into the parking lot. Nick was not in his truck or anywhere around the building.

"What is this place?"

Jason shook his head. "We've come this far. Let's have a look around…together."

She reached over, wrapping her fingers around his forearm. "I feel safe staying close to you."

He nodded. Her touch warmed him to the bone.

The two other cars parked and the drivers got out and headed around the side of the building without a backward glance at Jason's vehicle—which probably indicated that a lot of cars coming into the lot was expected. Something was going on inside that building.

"Okay." Jason pushed open his door as his heart skipped a beat. "Follow me."

Snow came down even harder as they hurried through the parking lot, ducking from car to car. Jason pressed against the side of the building with Isabel leaning against his back. They couldn't just walk in. They had no idea what they were facing.

The door popped open. Jason dived for the trees surrounding the property as a man dressed in a snowsuit headed in the other direction.

He signaled for Isabel to follow him, then skirted through the trees and bushes close to the building. If they could find a window, they might be able to peer inside and figure out what was going on in there. It didn't seem like the smuggling operation would be so aboveboard as to be operating out of a building.

They ran around to the far side of the building, still not finding any windows.

"Are you up to sneaking inside with me?"

She nodded. The door on the east side of the building was the only one no one had gone into or out of.

He reached for the handle and eased it open. He stared at metal shelving that ran from floor to ceiling containing boxes and what looked like auto parts. "I don't see anyone. Come on."

As Isabel placed her hand in his, he prayed he hadn't made a mistake in letting her come with him.

Isabel's heart pounded as they stepped inside what looked like a storage area for an auto-parts store. She could hear voices faint and indiscernible.

Jason held her hand as they rushed around the shelves of parts toward an open doorway. He signaled for her to crouch by the door while he got on the other side and peered out.

The three-story warehouse-like structure was built into the side of the hill, and they had actually stepped into the middle floor. One floor up was a glass wall that looked to be some sort of office. Two people, a man and a woman, were talking. The woman, dressed in a fur coat, threw back her head and laughed. Something about her seemed familiar. The man reached out and gathered the woman into his arms and kissed her. He was a broad-shouldered man with a belly. Judging from the gray hair, he was substantially older than the woman.

Isabel scooted over to where Jason was so she could look down below. If they had gone around to the final wall of the structure, it would have been obvious what they were dealing with. Down below on the ground floor were four huge garage doors and four snowplows. Men, including Nick, were standing around talking. Suited up and ready to get on the snowplows. One of the garage doors opened, and a man headed toward a plow, leaving Nick and two other guys. The rest of the ground floor looked like a repair shop with a scattering of tools and machines and one plow blade.

Jason whispered in her ear. "He's just going to work?"

"He takes odd jobs. Nothing permanent," she said. "So I guess this is a dead end." Disappointment colored her words. She wished she could place the woman in the glass office. Why did she look so familiar?

Nick glanced up in their direction. Her heart skipped a beat. She shrank back against the wall.

"We'd better get out of here." Jason hurried toward the door and Isabel was right behind him.

Jason pressed along the wall, preparing to ease around the corner if the coast was clear. He put a protective arm on her, letting her know it wasn't safe to go yet.

Several inches of snow had fallen in the short time they'd been up here. It was coming down fast and heavy.

Jason peered out again, then pressed his back against the metal wall. "They're starting to get busy. They didn't seem alarmed by our car. But I don't want to take a chance that they would know we didn't work here. I think this is a legit snowplow business but something still feels off to me. We should circle through the trees and then down into the parking lot."

That would take an extra ten minutes at least. Jason dived behind the bare brush that was part of the landscaping close to the building. Isabel followed as a man came around the corner from the parking lot.

He shone a light in her direction just as she dipped behind the bush. "So it's you. What are you doing here?" the man shouted.

Her heart beat faster. She'd glimpsed the man's face. "That's the guy with the gun from the Wilsons' house."

They both sprinted deeper into the trees, knowing that Mr. Gun would probably come after them.

It took only a moment before Isabel heard the footfalls behind her. Following the path Jason chose, staying close on his heels, she glanced over her shoulder at the dark figure pursuing them. The terrain became rockier as they ran past some large boulders. She could see her breath in the cold night air. Her legs pumped hard as they worked their way uphill.

Jason grabbed her and pulled her into a crevice between two boulders. She was so out of breath she was afraid the man would hear her inhaling and exhaling. The rock was hard and cold against her back as she faced Jason.

Were their tracks visible in the snow?

The crunch of footsteps landed on her ears. She took in only a shallow breath, fearing that the pursuer might see her breath.

The man turned a half circle, searching. Both of them slipped deeper into the crevice. She willed herself to be smaller.

Fear settled in around her, heavier than the snow falling from the sky. If Mr. Gun was at that warehouse too, there was something going on with that place other than snowplowing.

Mr. Gun spotted them and lunged in their direction. They slipped through the other side of the crevice and kept running. They were getting farther away from the warehouse. Would it even be safe to go back down to the parking lot? What choice did they have? They had to get out of here.

They ran for several more minutes before Jason glanced over his shoulder and then stopped, surveying the snowy hill below. They'd just come through an open area. "I think he gave up."

"I doubt it. He probably went back for reinforcements," she said.

"You're probably right. The fact that two people connected to a smuggling ring are working there can't be a coincidence," he said. "We need to get this information to someone we can trust."

That was a tall order. The men in the warehouse would probably be watching the parking lot by now. "How far away was that house we passed on the drive here?"

"It didn't seem that far when we were driving, but on foot—" Jason shook his head "—it could be an hour or more of walking."

"It's closer to get back to the parking lot. Maybe we can catch them with their guard down."

Her heart raced at the thought of plunging into the danger that awaited them. If the kingpin was one of the men in that building, he would be combing the mountain for them soon enough. The man in the glass office kissing the younger woman must be the owner or manager of the place. Was he the kingpin?

They ran along the ridgeline and then dived back down the mountain, passing another rock outcropping and coming out on an unplowed road. Isabel mulled over all they had seen. She slowed her steps. "I know who that woman was."

"The woman in the office?"

"Yes. I couldn't place her because she wasn't wearing the uniform, but it just clicked in my head. She was the maid who handed Nick that envelope. Whatever was in the envelope, he needed it before he got to the warehouse."

Jason nodded as though he were making sense of the information. "The guy with her was probably in charge of the snowplow business, maybe even the owner." Jason trudged along the unplowed road.

"They were clearly romantically involved. I don't know what it all means—maybe he has nothing to do with anything, but she does."

"Would maids have access to security codes?" Jason said.

"Yes, they would. And snowplow operators would know when a house was empty."

Before she could process all the conclusions they had come to, a mechanical roar filled the forest. A snowplow rounded a curve in the road. In the cab of the plow, Isabel could see Nick behind the wheel, barreling toward them.

EIGHTEEN

Jason turned and ran in the opposite direction as the snowplow loomed toward him. With Isabel right beside him, he searched the woods for a place to escape off the road.

The road had been cut into the side of a mountain. One side was sheer cliff and the other a steep rocky drop-off.

The rumble of the plow's motor was menacing. Isabel skirted toward the edge of the road and then jumped down the incline. Jason followed her down the steep slope.

Above them, the plow stopped. When he glanced up, Nick had gotten out of the cab and was stalking toward the edge of the road, holding a rifle. Jason grabbed Isabel and pulled her behind a boulder. The first shot glanced off the rock just above their heads.

He surveyed the area around them. Nick would probably chase them down the mountain on foot. The incline was steep and treacherous. He pointed to the next rock they needed to make it to for cover. Half crouching and half running, they dived toward the boulder.

He caught a flash of movement in his peripheral vision, the reflective material on Nick's snowsuit. Nick had not left the road yet. The rifle had substantial range, hundreds of yards.

Jason huddled down behind the rock. Isabel pressed close to him. He couldn't see anything below him that would shield them. They'd have to move sideways, which meant they were still within rifle range.

"He can't shoot at both of us at the same time. I'll go first. Then you run and get behind that outcropping as fast as you can." He pointed. "I'll get to you as soon as I can."

She tore off her glove and pressed a hand to his cheek. Her round brown eyes filled with warmth. "You're making yourself a target…for me."

"It'll be okay." Her touch, the softness in her expression, drew him in and warmed him to the marrow of his bones.

"You could die. I don't want you to die."

He kissed her forehead and then her lips. He loved her. In that moment, he knew that he loved her. Even if they couldn't be together, he loved her. "I don't want to die either but this is the best way for us to get a safe distance from him. We have to work our way down the mountain and get out of rifle range." The plan was not foolproof. Nick still might choose to follow them.

Another rifle shot reverberated through the forest, stirring up snow close to the rock. They both crouched lower.

"After I go, count to three and then run as fast as you can."

She nodded.

Jason burst up from the rock and ran in a zigzag pattern, jumping around the smaller rocks. Two rifle shots zinged past him, one so close that the displaced air pummeled his eardrum. He dived to the ground.

He caught a flash of color below him. Isabel had chosen to go toward a cluster of trees instead of the outcropping. Another shot shattered the silence of the wild. It was aimed at her. From where he lay on the ground, he prayed that the shot had missed her.

She disappeared into the cluster of trees.

Using the moment it would take Nick to reorient himself, Jason burst up from the ground and darted toward the shelter of the trees. He glanced to his side. Nick had worked his way down the mountain by maybe ten yards. He'd have to stop to line up another shot.

Jason could see the trees up ahead and spotted Isabel's jacket again. His foot hooked on a rock and he stumbled and fell facedown into the snow. The fall shocked and disoriented him. His brain told him he needed to stand up and to keep running, but his body remained unresponsive.

Isabel emerged from the trees, reaching out to pull him to his feet. Another shot sounded. So close. They hurried toward the shelter of the trees five yards away.

Another shot echoed down the mountain, breaking a branch above them. Birds fluttered into the sky. Jason grabbed Isabel and held her close.

"Don't do that ever again. You could have died."

She nestled against his chest. "I didn't want to lose you, Jason."

More than anything, he wished they could remain suspended in the moment. He wanted to hold her forever. He kissed the top of her head. "Not if I can help it."

A groaning noise reached his ears, followed by a thud: Nick's feet as he jumped off a large rock, making his way down toward them.

"We have to keep moving." Jason peered through the trees, searching for their next point of cover. It was dark enough that most objects were only shadows.

"What if we worked our way back up to the road and got to that plow?" she said.

"It's worth a try. Move parallel to the road for a while, so he doesn't figure out what we're doing," whispered Jason.

Through the trees, he could see Nick turning from side to side, searching the landscape for them. The glint of the rifle caught in the moonlight.

They sprinted from one rock outcropping to another, from brush to clusters of trees. Twice, rifle shots zinged over their heads, forcing them to drop to the ground and crawl.

Jason gasped for breath as they ran toward a boulder closer to the road. He could see the edge of the road just above him. Isabel kept pace with him as they half ran, half climbed up to the road.

Once they were on the level footing of the road, he leaned over, resting his hands on his knees to catch his breath. It had been at least ten minutes since a shot was fired. He didn't see Nick anywhere down below.

Isabel patted her heart and took in a quick breath. She glanced nervously down the steep incline, shaking her head. "He doesn't give up easily."

As crazy as Nick was, he seemed to have the stalking instincts of a lion.

Once his breath slowed, Jason pivoted and jogged down the road with Isabel beside him.

His leg muscles strained from all the running and climbing they'd done. They rounded one curve and then another. Still no sign of the plow. They must be getting close.

Jason slowed down enough to talk. "He may be waiting for us at the plow, suspecting that we would try to get to it."

Most of the landscape was repetitive. It was hard to know how close they were.

Isabel shot ahead of him. "I see snowplow tracks down there."

He saw them now too, but no snowplow. When they got to the tracks, it was clear that Nick had backed the plow up until he came to a place where he could turn around and head back down the road.

"So much for that plan." Isabel slumped down onto a tree stump beside the road.

The plow probably had a radio in it. Had he been told to get back to work? Or maybe he'd just decided to leave them to the elements for now. How far were they from shelter?

"This road has to lead somewhere."

"Can I rest for a minute?" she said.

He could tell from her tone of voice she was giving up hope.

"Sure." He paced down the road, looking for smoke rising in the air from a woodstove or lights, any sign of civilization. He didn't see anything but trees and rock.

It was a sure bet that whoever was behind all the smuggling wouldn't risk their getting back to civilization. Sooner or later, someone would come looking for them to kill them.

From the tree stump where she sat, Isabel tilted her head. Clouds slipped over the moon, making it darker. The snowfall had stopped at least.

Sitting still made her feel the cold more intensely. She rose to her feet and rubbed her arms, pushing the despair that plagued her to the back of her mind. No matter what, she needed to not give up hope. They couldn't be that far from a place where they could find help and shelter.

Jason returned and held out a gloved hand for her to take. "Let's head down the road. We're bound to run into something or someone."

"I suppose that's what we should do." She couldn't hide the weariness in her voice.

Jason scanned the area above them as though he were looking for potential threats. Then he looked at her. His eyes filled with compassion. "It's the best plan I have for now."

They were both exhausted and cold, but being with Jason somehow made it bearable.

They ran for what felt like miles. The ground

leveled out. They passed an area that was fenced off with barbed wire, but there were no cows or ranchers, no sign of life anywhere.

They drank from a mountain stream, the water icy cold as she cupped it in her hands. Isabel stood up from the creek and put her hands on her hips. With the terrain so flat, she could see for miles and still there was no sign of people.

"I guess we were pushed farther back into the hills than I realized."

They heard the sound of a vehicle on the road before they saw the headlights. Any noise echoed in the quiet. Both of them moved toward some brush and crouched. If it was someone who could help them, they'd have a hard time catching up to him, but they couldn't risk being spotted if Nick or one of his cohorts came looking for them.

The battered old truck came around the bend and stopped. A man got out and peered down the road, shining a flashlight. Their tracks where they'd made their way down to the mountain stream were clearly visible.

"It's not Nick. Not his build." The truck hadn't been one of the ones in the parking lot at the snowplow facility.

Isabel jumped to her feet and waved. "Hey." She ran across the field as the man took notice of her.

Jason followed her.

She hollered as the man came to the edge of the road. "Boy, are we glad to see you."

The man was maybe thirty years old. Fringes of red hair peeked out from beneath a knit cap. He pointed across the field. "Saw your tracks. Not many people come up Copper Junction Road. You folks break down or something?"

"You could say that. Could you give us a ride back into town or at least some place where we can phone for someone to come pick us up?"

The man pulled his hat off and rubbed his hair. He wasn't wearing gloves. "Sure. I can do that."

They made their way up the hill. Isabel got into the cab first. Jason squeezed in by the passenger-side door of the old truck as he and the man made small talk about fishing and hunting.

The truck lumbered down the road until they came to a crossroads and took a right turn.

Isabel tensed. Maybe she'd gotten all turned around when they were running away, but it seemed like town was in the other direction.

"There's a little gas station up the road where you folks will be able to make your phone call," said the man as though he had read her mind.

Maybe because they'd been running for so long and seen the dark side of humanity, her trust in the goodness of people had been dismantled. She couldn't let go of the feeling that something wasn't right.

The man continued to drive down a two-lane that didn't connect with a main road.

Isabel squeezed Jason's leg just above the knee to get his attention. She raised her eyebrows, hoping he would indicate that he felt the same uneasiness.

Jason kept talking about where the best fishing holes were, but he pressed his shoulder a little harder against hers.

The bleak unsettled landscape rolled by.

"How far did you say it was to that gas station?" She hoped her voice didn't give away the fear that had taken up residence in her body.

"Oh, just up the road a piece." The man shifted gears.

They came up over a hill.

Terror crashed through Isabel.

Down below was the warehouse with the snowplows. The man reached into the side compartment of the door and pulled out a pistol, which he aimed at Isabel. His voice grew sinister and dark. "Don't think about jumping out or fighting back. I'll shoot her faster than you can blink."

The truck rolled down the hill so fast, it would have been dangerous to try to escape. The parking lot was empty except for one car.

Theirs was nowhere in sight and Nick's black truck was gone.

Isabel's heart pounded against her rib cage. The man parked the truck, still pointing the gun at her. "Now we're going to go inside. No funny business. Got that?"

They both nodded.

"I'll get out of the cab first, understand," the redheaded man said.

She stared at the barrel of the gun and nodded. Her hands were trembling, and her mouth had gone completely dry.

The man pulled the keys out of the ignition. He smiled. This time she saw the darkness behind his eyes. "Just in case you were going to try something."

Snow swirled lightly out of the sky as the man marched them into the warehouse. Isabel glanced at Jason, trying to read his expression. It was two against one, even if one had a gun.

Jason lifted his head in a nod, indicating that they should try to take the man with the gun.

Isabel stopped.

"Keep moving." The redheaded man aimed the gun at her.

Jason used the moment of distraction to whirl around and kick the gun out of the man's hand. It flew, landing in deep snow. While she ran to find the gun, Isabel heard the slap of skin against skin as the men exchanged blows.

Heart racing, she scanned the snow for the gun while the men continued to fight.

Then she heard it. The click of a shotgun shell being ratcheted into the chamber. "Put your hands in the air."

She turned, staring into the cold eyes of the short muscular man who had come after her at the Wilsons' house. Mr. Gun.

"You too." The short man aimed the gun at Jason.

The redheaded man scrambled in the snow to retrieve his handgun and then pointed it at Isabel.

"I told you not to try anything funny," he said between gasps for air.

Jason and Isabel marched side by side. She wasn't about to give up. There had to be a way to get free. The man with the handgun ran ahead and opened the door. Just outside the glass-walled office, they stepped out onto a mezzanine that provided a view of the entire facility.

All the plows were back in place. There was no one behind the glass of the office or down below by the plows.

The men led them down to the room where the snowplow parts were stored and commanded them to sit on the floor with their backs to each other. The redhead bound their hands and gagged their mouths with duct tape and tied the two of them together with rope back to back.

"Now, you just sit tight until the boss gets back. He can decide what to do with you." The man traced a finger down Isabel's cheek. "At which time, I get to collect a bonus for finding you."

He winked at Isabel, rose to his feet and slipped out the door. Mr. Gun followed. The door closed. As far as she could see, there were only two men in the facility right now. If they could get out of this room, they might be able to escape.

Jason wriggled, struggling to break free. Isabel twisted her hands, hoping to loosen the duct tape that bound them. Her wrists hurt from the effort.

After a moment of stillness, his head brushed against the back of hers as he studied his surroundings. He scooted across the floor toward the metal shelves that held the motor parts. Isabel pushed with her feet to move with him. He must have seen something on the shelf that might help them escape.

She had no idea what his plan was or when "the boss" would return and decide how to kill them. She had no doubt their death was imminent if they didn't find a way to escape their captors and get to one of those vehicles.

NINETEEN

Jason had spotted a piece of metal protruding from one of the lower shelves. He might be able to cut himself free and then remove the duct tape from Isabel, as well. He lifted his hands, which were tied in front of him, and scraped the tape along the metal.

Even though he had no idea if they had ten minutes to escape or ten hours, a sense of urgency made it feel like there was a weight on his chest. He sawed back and forth as the layers of duct tape were cut away. He was nearly free when he heard footsteps outside the room.

They both scooted back across the floor to where they had been put. Jason pressed the cut tape back around his wrists and held his hands as though they were still bound. The door burst open and the redheaded man stepped in.

He crossed his arms over his chest. "Boss is back. Just a few minutes and we'll get this mess wrapped up." The man punched his fist against his palm and narrowed his eyes. His expression chilled Jason to the bone.

The man grinned. "Don't go anywhere now." He laughed, shaking his head. "I crack myself up." He closed the door.

Jason listened to the man's boots pounding on the concrete floor before twisting free of the rope that bound him to Isabel. He tore the gag off his mouth, and then, still crouching, he came to help Isabel. She stared up at him. He touched the corner of the duct tape on her mouth. "This will hurt."

She nodded, her eyes filled with trust. He ripped it off in one quick motion. A tiny gasp escaped her lips.

He tried to peel the tape off her hands. He pulled, winding the layers of tape off her wrists until she was free.

He ran to the outside door they had used when they first entered the building. Locked.

"Let's see if we can find another way out." They wove through the shelves that reached up to the high ceiling until they found a back door. The door opened to a landing and a stairwell leading upward.

It was too much to hope that it would lead them straight outside.

He pressed against the wall and stepped lightly up the stairs. Isabel touched his arm as she stood one step below him. At the top of the stairs, he eased the door open slowly.

Raised voices drifted down a hallway. He slipped through the door, not daring to open it all the way, and then he crouched on the carpet. They must be in the hallway behind the glass-walled office.

Three men were arguing. The only voice he recognized was Nick's.

He couldn't pick up all the conversation. It sounded like an argument over money for a job they'd just done. Thundering footsteps came up the hallway into the office as the voice of the man who had tied them up blasted through the room. "They've escaped."

Jason angled around the corner just in time to see three men running out of the office. Nick, the man who had been kissing the maid and a third man—Larry, the FBI agent who had picked them up when they'd escaped from the Wilsons' house. Now they knew who the turn-coat was.

All the men ran in the opposite direction of where Isabel and he were hiding. The fourth man, the redhead, trailed behind. He waited until he heard the sound of the slamming door and moved toward the office. Isabel grabbed his arm. "What are you doing?"

"There's probably a phone in there." He

stepped into the empty office and she entered behind him. "We can call Michael now. He's not the turncoat."

"I don't think we have time to wait for help. We should get out of here."

Her thinking was clearer than his.

"I'm sure they will send a man out to the parking lot to make sure we can't get to those cars."

Light came into Isabel's eyes. "The snow-plows. They won't be expecting us to use one of the snowplows."

He peered through the glass wall of the office. Down below, a man ran by. Jason and Isabel crouched out of view but where they were still able to watch the activity. The man looked from side to side and then took a door that led to the parking lot.

They heard the thunder of footsteps up metal stairs.

They needed to get out of here and fast. The door they'd come through led back to the parts storage room. Jason ran down the hallway and tried another door that had stairs leading down. Just as he closed the door he heard voices in the hallway headed back toward the office.

There were at least five men in all. The three who had been in the office and two who had tied them up. He had to assume that at least one of those men would remain in the glass office watching the snowplow area. This plan was fraught with risk, but it was the best they had. The stairs opened up on the floor where the plows were. Jason pressed against a wall by the door so shadows covered him.

Sure enough, the man who must be the boss or owner, and was probably the mastermind behind all the smuggling, stared down from his office. Even if they stayed close to the wall, there was a ten-foot stretch where they'd be spotted before they could hide behind one of the plows.

Isabel remained at the base of the stairs, door slightly ajar, waiting for the signal from him. He could just make out her face in the little slit where the door was open.

Jason tilted his head and watched the man above them, waiting for a second of distraction when he and Isabel could traverse the area where they'd be visible.

The seconds ticked by. The man continued to survey the area below. Jason became aware of the hardness of the wall against his back, of his own breathing and of Isabel perched behind the partly open door, her gaze fixed on him.

Finally the short muscular man, Mr. Gun, came into the office and the owner turned his back to Jason.

Jason bolted toward the first snowplow. The

soft padding of Isabel's footsteps behind him pressed on his ears. He crouched in front of the machine in between the plow blade and the garage door. Easing around to the side, he glanced up. The owner was staring out the office window again. Jason shrank back into the shadows as his heart pounded out an erratic beat. No way could he climb into the cab and not be spotted. That meant they would have only seconds to get out of the warehouse before someone would be on their tail.

He slipped back around to the front of the plow by the blade where Isabel still hid.

She leaned close and whispered in his ear. "The plow on the end doesn't have any lights shining on it."

He peered down the line of plow blades before nodding that her idea was the most viable one. They scurried from one plow to the next. He eased open the cab door of the last plow. Isabel got in after him on the other side.

He stared down at the control panel, trying to get his bearings, grateful to see that the key was in the ignition.

"The garage door. There's a switch." Before he could say anything, she had jumped out of the cab and headed toward the wall.

He started the vehicle as the door eased open and Isabel raced to get back in the cab. Now for sure they'd be noticed. He eased the plow forward even before the door was all the way open.

Isabel grabbed hold of the door and tried to climb into the cab as the tracks of the plow rolled forward. He reached out a hand and pulled her in.

Two men were behind them. One jumped onto the cab of the plow.

Jason hit the accelerator as the plow eased forward onto the flat area outside the garage doors. Another garage door opened, and the lights of a second plow glared out at them.

Jason gained speed, climbing the hill toward the road. He chose the steeper terrain, hoping that would get rid of the unwanted guest clinging to the outside of the cab.

The man jumped off. Jason caught a glimpse of movement as the man raised a gun.

"Get down." He threw a protective hand over Isabel. Gunfire shattered the glass of the cab and rained down on them. His skin stung where the glass cut him. A chilly breeze blew in around them.

The plow lumbered up to the road that led back into town. Top speed looked to be about thirty miles an hour.

The other plow slipped in behind them.

Isabel sat back up, craning her neck. "Nick is in the other plow."

Jason pressed the gas pedal to the floor, wishing they could go faster. He turned out onto the main road. One of the cars from the warehouse passed him and then slowed to a crawl. Nick was still bearing down on them in the plow.

"They're trying to box us in." Jason stared at the road ahead, where a car was coming toward them. He couldn't risk the life of an innocent person.

He eased off the gas.

The car going in the opposite direction whizzed by.

Metal scraped against metal as Nick rammed into the back of them. Both of them jostled around in their seats.

Jason pressed the gas, turned the wheel and prepared to ease around the slow car in front of him. The car edged onto the wrong side of the road.

"Fine—that's how you're gonna play it?" Jason jerked the wheel in the other direction. The blade collided with the car as Jason pushed him toward a ditch.

The car was no match for the power of the plow. With one final push, the car slid into a snowbank. But Nick still rolled toward them.

Nick rammed against the side of them with the blade raised.

Jason pressed the accelerator and cranked the

wheel as the other plow pushed them down the road sideways. He disentangled his plow from Nick's.

Jason rolled forward off the road to get away from Nick. The tracks of the plow bit through the snow as they lumbered up a hill and down the other side. Nick was right behind them.

The hill grew steeper. The plow listed to one side.

"We're going to tip over." Isabel's fear-filled words seemed to come from far away as he struggled to get the machine onto stable ground.

The plow rolled over on its side, and Isabel fell on top of him.

The motor was still running. Tiny gasps escaped Isabel's lips as she struggled to right herself. She climbed out the back of the cab's broken window.

Jason pushed himself up. His hands were bleeding from the broken glass. He pulled himself through the same opening Isabel had used. Isabel jumped down into the snow.

Nick was maybe twenty feet from them, still behind the wheel of the other plow. The headlights glared at them.

Isabel took off running before Jason had jumped down off the plow. Drops of blood in the snow revealed that she was cut up, as well.

He raced after her as the plow drew closer, the engine noise surrounding them.

Isabel felt the warm seep of blood on her forehead as she struggled to navigate through the deep snow.

The clanging of the plow's motor stopped. She looked over her shoulder. Not wanting to risk the same outcome as their plow, Nick had turned the motor off and was crawling out of the cab. He held a gun in his hand.

Jason was at least twenty yards behind her and struggling even more than she was. She lifted her feet one after the other as she slogged up the snowy hillside. When this was over—if they survived—she never wanted to trudge through snow again.

A gunshot echoed across the terrain. She winced but kept moving, trusting that Jason would catch up with her.

She was nearly to the tree line when she looked over her shoulder. Jason was lying face-down on the ground.

Her heart stopped. She was out of pistol range, but if she ran back to help him, she would be a target too.

She turned and hurried back down the hill toward Jason. If they both died out here today, fine. She wasn't about to abandon a good man to the forces of evil. Before she could get to him, Jason rose to his feet. His hands were bloody and he'd left stains in the snow.

He signaled for her to keep running. Nick was having as much trouble navigating the deep snow as they were. The only way he could aim a shot was to stop moving.

She heard another bullet whiz through the air just as she reached the tree line. She slowed, looking behind her for Jason.

Finding a large tree with long branches, she hid underneath it, peering out and hoping to see Jason's boots. She caught her breath as the minutes ticked by. She heard a rustling off to the side and a moment later saw Nick's dark boots moving past.

What was going on here? Where was Jason?

She rolled out from underneath the tree and headed back toward the tree line. Down below, Jason had crawled into the cab of the working plow. He must have doubled back once Nick entered the trees and had no view of the plow. He signaled for her to come back down.

Her feet sank three feet down as she struggled to get to Jason. A pistol shot zinged past, close enough to send shock waves through her. She heard groaning behind her. Nick had fallen in the deep snow.

Jason got out of the cab and waved his arm,

indicating she should get down the hill. The pistol rested on the surface of the snow.

Once and for all, she would see to it that Nick Solomon wouldn't escape justice ever again. She hurried toward the gun and picked it up.

"Get on your feet." Her voice held unexpected strength.

Nick pushed himself up. He was covered in snow. "Oh, come on. You're not going to shoot, Blondie."

"Try me." She aimed the pistol close to Nick's feet and squeezed the trigger.

"Whoa." Shock spread across Nick's face as he did a jig with his feet and held his hands up in surrender.

She could never shoot anyone. Nick just needed to know who was in control now. "My name is not Blondie. It's Isabel."

Jason came up behind her. "Turn around and put your hands behind your back." Jason held a scarf that he must have found in the cab of the plow.

Nick sneered. Isabel raised the pistol and pointed it at him. Nick glared but turned his back to them and put his hands together behind him.

They led Nick down the hill with his hands bound. Isabel held the gun while Jason drove.

Once they were out on the road, he checked the rearview mirror several times.

Both of them knew there was a good possibility that the others from the warehouse were after them.

Isabel felt a sense of satisfaction as Nick hung his head and closed his eyes. "I'm telling you, baby, you and me would have made a great team."

"I don't want to be on that kind of team." She glanced at Jason, feeling warmth spread over her as he gazed at her before focusing on the road.

She cared deeply for him. They had been through so much together. He had shown over and over that he would give up his life for her. What was going to happen now that all of this was close to being over?

TWENTY

Jason and Isabel sat in the FBI field office waiting to be debriefed after a trip to the emergency room to deal with their cuts. The head of the smuggling ring had opted not to chase them. Knowing that he'd been found out, he had booked a ticket to Argentina along with his girlfriend, the maid. Agents had caught him at the airport.

Michael came out of his office. "We'll need to interview each of you separately."

Isabel's hand grasped his. "I'll go first." She squeezed his fingers.

He saw an affection in her eyes that made his heart race. Still, was the attraction just because they had needed each other so desperately to stay alive or was there something deeper there that could survive their return to ordinary life?

He had opened his heart to her but old fears returned. He didn't want to end up like his father, a broken man. Women left, they betrayed—that was what they did. He picked up a magazine and flipped through it. Maybe Isabel was different...maybe.

Ten minutes later, Isabel emerged from the office. Her round doe eyes rested on him. "Your turn. I've got to get over to the office and explain things to Mary." She reached out and squeezed his hand. "I guess this is it."

He took in a breath. Should he say something about how he felt but how the doubts plagued him? "Yes, maybe I'll see you around."

A shadow seemed to fall across her face. "Sure. That would be nice." Was that disappointment that tainted her words?

Michael came out of his office and stood in the doorway watching them.

Jason stepped toward Michael's office as the door to the outside opened and closed—Isabel was gone.

"You two have been through quite an ordeal together," said Michael, turning to position himself behind his desk.

"Yes. Yes, we have." Jason nodded.

He stepped inside Michael's office and closed the door.

Michael clicked the keyboard of his laptop. "It seems our rogue agent has decided to run too, but I suspect it will just be a matter of hours before we have him in custody."

"And the other men we saw at the warehouse?"

"Isabel was able to identify them. Petty criminals. The locals can pick them up and bring them in."

Jason turned sideways and stared at the door, thinking about Isabel stepping outside. "So they're not in custody yet. What if they come after her for revenge?"

"They don't have the economic resources to flee. It's just a matter of hours before we pick them up. You can stay with her for a little longer, can't you?"

"Give me a minute." Jason jumped up from his chair and bolted for the door. He took the stairs two at a time and raced out to the street.

Isabel was already two blocks away, walking into a headwind with her head down and her arms crossed. He ran to catch up with her, calling out her name when he was a block away.

She turned to face him.

"Jason, what is it?"

"You know the two men that came after you at the Wilsons' are still at large and the red-headed guy."

"Michael mentioned it. They don't want to get caught. I'm sure they're hiding," she said.

He shifted his weight from one foot to the other. "Why take a chance? What's another day or two together, watching each other's backs?"

"Jason, is that really why you ran all the way up the street?"

"Yes. I'm worried about your safety."

Her expression drooped. Her brown eyes glazed. "Oh, is that all?"

He reached his hand out to her. "Isabel, I didn't mean to make you cry."

"When I saw you coming up the street I thought that maybe… I don't know… That it wasn't about this whole smuggling thing. That you were coming after me to be with me, just to be with me."

The vulnerability in her voice floored him. He let out a breath and shook his head.

"What?" A faint smile graced her face as she leaned closer to him.

"Guess I was telling myself a lie. I was looking for an excuse to be with you. Isabel?" He knew he loved her. Why was it so hard for him to admit that?

"Yes?" she said.

He pulled his gloves off and tossed them on the ground. Then he inched her gloves off, as well, so he could hold her hands in his. "Isabel Connor. I do want to be with you. Not just for another day until those men are picked up but for the rest of my life."

She bounced from toe to heel. Her face

brightening. "Yes. I want that too. I want to be your wife."

"Well then, there you have it. I love you, Isabel."

"I love you, Jason."

He leaned in and kissed her with the snow swirling around them and the early-morning sun shining on them.

* * * * *

*If you loved this story,
don't miss these other exciting books
from Sharon Dunn:*

*COLD CASE JUSTICE
MISTAKEN TARGET
FATAL VENDETTA
BIG SKY SHOWDOWN*

*Find more great reads at
www.LoveInspired.com.*

Dear Reader,

I hope you enjoyed the dangerous and romantic adventure that Jason and Isabel went on to see to it that justice was served. Isabel is probably one of my favorite characters so far. She comes from a difficult childhood and made some destructive choices as a teenager. Yet her faith shines like the morning sun. I love the way Isabel clings to God and His unconditional love no matter what. All of us have done and said things that we deeply regret. Like Isabel, it is easy for me to feel shame over past choices. I have to be so careful that I do not fixate on those past choices because they will consume me. To me the remedy is to keep my eyes in the right place, on God and His faithfulness. This is a moment-by-moment choice sometimes. When Isabel starts to beat herself up in her head, she prays, hums a hymn or says a Bible verse. All of these things help me too. May your faith shine like the morning sun and may you rest your gaze on what matters most.

Sharon Dunn

Get 4 FREE REWARDS!

We'll send you 2 FREE Books <u>plus</u> 2 FREE Mystery Gifts.

Love Inspired® Suspense books feature Christian characters facing challenges to their faith... and lives.

FREE Value Over **$20**

YES! Please send me 2 FREE Love Inspired® Suspense novels and my 2 FREE mystery gifts (gifts are worth about $10 retail). After receiving them, if I don't wish to receive any more books, I can return the shipping statement marked "cancel." If I don't cancel, I will receive 4 brand-new novels every month and be billed just $5.24 each for the regular-print edition or $5.74 each for the larger-print edition in the U.S., or $5.74 each for the regular-print edition or $6.24 each for the larger-print edition in Canada. That's a savings of at least 13% off the cover price. It's quite a bargain! Shipping and handling is just 50¢ per book in the U.S. and 75¢ per book in Canada*. I understand that accepting the 2 free books and gifts places me under no obligation to buy anything. I can always return a shipment and cancel at any time. The free books and gifts are mine to keep no matter what I decide.

Choose one: ☐ **Love Inspired® Suspense**
Regular-Print
(153/353 IDN GMY5)

☐ **Love Inspired® Suspense**
Larger-Print
(107/307 IDN GMY5)

Name (please print)

Address   Apt. #

City   State/Province   Zip/Postal Code

Mail to the Reader Service:
IN U.S.A.: P.O. Box 1341, Buffalo, NY 14240-8531
IN CANADA: P.O. Box 603, Fort Erie, Ontario L2A 5X3

Want to try two free books from another series? Call 1-800-873-8635 or visit www.ReaderService.com.

LIS18

Get 4 FREE REWARDS!

We'll send you 2 FREE Books plus 2 FREE Mystery Gifts.

Harlequin® Heartwarming™ Larger-Print books feature traditional values of home, family, community and most of all—love.

FREE
Value Over
$20

YES! Please send me the **Home on the Ranch Collection** in Larger Print. This collection begins with 3 FREE books and 2 FREE gifts in the first shipment. Along with my 3 free books, I'll also get the next 4 books from the Home on the Ranch Collection, in LARGER PRINT, which I may either return and owe nothing, or keep for the low price of $5.24 U.S./ $5.89 CDN each plus $2.99 for shipping and handling per shipment*. If I decide to continue, about once a month for 8 months I will get 6 or 7 more books, but will only need to pay for 4. That means 2 or 3 books in every shipment will be FREE! If I decide to keep the entire collection, I'll have paid for only 32 books because 19 books are FREE! I understand that accepting the 3 free books and gifts places me under no obligation to buy anything. I can always return a shipment and cancel at any time. My free books and gifts are mine to keep no matter what I decide.

268 HCN 3760 468 HCN 3760

Name	(PLEASE PRINT)	
Address		Apt. #
City	State/Prov.	Zip/Postal Code

Signature (if under 18, a parent or guardian must sign)

Mail to the **Reader Service:**

IN U.S.A.: P.O. Box 1867, Buffalo, NY. 14240-1867
IN CANADA: P.O. Box 609, Fort Erie, Ontario L2A 5X3

* Terms and prices subject to change without notice. Prices do not include applicable taxes. Sales tax applicable in NY. Canadian residents will be charged applicable taxes. This offer is limited to one order per household. All orders subject to approval. Credit or debit balances in a customer's account(s) may be offset by any other outstanding balance owed by or to the customer. Please allow 3 to 4 weeks for delivery. Offer available while quantities last. Offer not available to Quebec residents.

READERSERVICE.COM

Manage your account online!

- Review your order history
- Manage your payments
- Update your address

*We've designed the
Reader Service website
just for you.*

Enjoy all the features!

- Discover new series available to you, and read excerpts from any series.
- Respond to mailings and special monthly offers.
- Browse the Bonus Bucks catalog and online-only exculsives.
- Share your feedback.

Visit us at:

ReaderService.com